IN THE
ARMS OF A
Savage

K.L. HALL

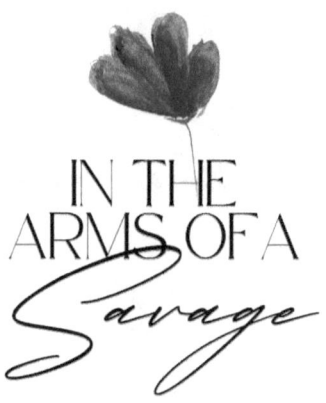

IN THE
ARMS OF A
Savage

K.L. HALL

Dedication

To all the good girls... stay golden.
-K.L. Hall

Acknowledgments

Wow! This is book number fifteen! Sometimes I still can't believe it. As many of you know, I started publishing in 2013, and I must say that this has been one hell of a journey over the past four years. For those of you who have been supporting me since book one, I thank you from the bottom of my heart. Thank you all for your motivation and your kind words of encouragement.

    -K.L. Hall

Epigraph

Synopsis

All Raquel Valentine wanted was a carefree Miami girl's trip to celebrate her college graduation. But, when a man is gunned down right in front of her, and she captures it on her phone, she instantly becomes the Calloway family's newest target, plunging her into a world of danger and uncertainty.

Andreas "Law" Calloway is more than a drug dealer. He's a disrespectful savage and the new head of his family's empire. He knows the streets like the back of his hand, and now that he's got the world at his fingertips, his first order of business is to wreak havoc on those responsible for his older brother's death.

When Law decides to spare Raquel's life, he does so with one stipulation: making sure she doesn't talk to the police. He never thought he'd find himself caught between what his mind knows and what his heart wants. Soon, he finds himself drawn to Raquel in a way he can't explain. The chemistry between them is too strong for either to deny. Raquel knows that her survival comes at a cost. Will being around Law turn her heart of gold into the heart of a savage?

CHAPTER ONE
Raquel

On the night of my graduation, I sat outside my apartment in the driver's seat of my 2009 Honda Civic contemplating. Both hands were wrapped tightly around the steering wheel as I replayed the voicemail over and over in my head. I glanced over at the engagement ring with the small diamond inside of it wrapped around my finger and wiped the tear that was gently sliding down my face. I didn't know if I was broken, angry, or a mixture of both. There I was, ready to marry my high school sweetheart, Derrick, and he'd butt dialed me as he let some whore give him head. The worst part was it wasn't just any whore. I'd heard her voice a million times before over the past four years. He was messing around with my room-mate, Yasmine.

I didn't know what to do. At that point, I needed more than a box of tissues and a comforting hug. One part of me was telling me to go in the house and slap fire from anything and anybody that moved. The other part just wanted to crawl up into the fetal position and cry for the rest of my life. I decided to go with the first part. I didn't know what I was going to see, but I stepped outside of my car, slammed the door behind me, and ran up the two flights of steps to my apartment. My hand was shaking as I attempted to put the key into the lock. *Get it together, Raquel*, I told myself as I slowly turned the doorknob.

As soon as I took my first step, my ears were greeted with sounds of R. Kelly crooning from the Bluetooth speaker in the living room. Those motherfuckers were really trying to set the mood. My eyes landed on a pair of black lace panties in the hallway along with Derrick's shoes by the door and his pants not too far from them. I could feel my heart pumping a million miles a minute with every step I took down the hallway. The closer I got to Yasmine's room, the more her moans started to drown out the second verse of "It Seems like You're Ready." My ears were no stranger to the sounds of her moans, but I never *ever* thought I'd hear them when Derrick was around. I put my sweaty hand on the knob to her bedroom, and with every ounce of strength in me, I swung the door open.

"Oooh fuck, baby. That's it right there," Yasmine moaned as she rode Derrick's dick.

"Mmm... You like that shit?" he asked as he smacked her ass.

"Hell yeah. I do," she moaned.

"What the fuck!" I yelled as I watched Yasmine riding Derrick's dick up and down like a carousel. His hands were wrapped tightly around her waist as she gyrated on top of him, still moaning... still fucking.

"Oh shit!" Derrick yelled when he got a glimpse of me standing in the doorway.

Yasmine turned around and screamed as if she were the star in a horror movie. She quickly climbed off Derrick and ran to put on a t-shirt to cover her pierced nipples. I stood frozen in my steps, gawking at them. I couldn't fight. I couldn't move. I could barely breathe. Not only was Derrick cheating with my room-mate, they were fucking like professional porn stars. That only meant one thing to me. I was the only one in that apartment still holding onto my virginity.

"Baby, listen. It's not what it looks like!" Derrick yelled as he jumped up to put his boxers back on and then stood in front of me, trying to grab my hands.

I swatted him away and pushed him back.

"What the fuck do you mean it's not what the fuck it looks like, Derrick? Huh? So I didn't just catch you fucking my room-mate?" I yelled.

"Raquel, please just listen. Just hear me out, okay? Let me explain!"

"Let you explain what? I saved myself for you, Derrick! How could you do this to me?" I yelled as tears streamed down my eyes.

I glanced over at Yasmine with tears as hot as fire still streaming down my face. She was standing in the corner of her room, shaking. Without saying a word, I walked over to her and slapped her hard across the face.

"You fucking bitch! How could you do this to me?"

Yasmine wailed out in pain and held her face.

"What the fuck is wrong with the both of you! We were supposed to get married in six months! Six fucking months! You were supposed to be my fucking maid of honor, bitch!" I screamed at the both of them while staring at her.

"Raqi, I'm so sorry. I never meant to hurt you," Yasmine pleaded.

"Shut the fuck up and get out before I start shutting shit down in this bitch!" I yelled with no remorse in my voice. "Both of you!"

I pushed Derrick out of the room, down the hall, and out the front door with just his boxers on. I threw his shoes, shirt, and jeans out one by one to make him fetch them like the dog he was. Before I could get to her, Yasmine ran out the door behind him in just a T-shirt. I slammed the door behind them and realized I was breathing heavy as if I'd just run a marathon. I knew my heart rate and blood pressure were probably through the roof. I stood there alone. I didn't know what to do. I paced the living room floor before running over to smash the Bluetooth speaker on the hardwood floor to cease the slow jams.

"Fucking bitch!" I screamed and pulled out my cell phone to call my best friend, Camille, on FaceTime.

"Hello?" she answered.

"Camille..."

"Raqi? What's wrong? What's going on?" she asked, staring at me.

"I... I just..."

"You what? Raquel, you're scaring me."

"I just caught Derrick fucking Yasmine," I said before the waterworks started flowing all over again.

"Oh shit," she muttered into the receiver.

I looked at the screen and saw her cover her mouth as her eyes widened.

"Yeah. 'Oh shit' is right," I scoffed and wiped my tears.

"I knew that ho was a mothafuckin' ho! Ughhhhh!"

"She's as ho-ish as they come, too." I nodded.

"What the fuck do you wanna do? You know I'm ready to beat any and everybody ass! And Derrick! How fucking dare he! You two were supposed to get fucking married!" she screamed.

"In six fucking months, Camille! And he pulls this shit?"

"So, what are you going to do, girl?"

"What can I do? What's done is done now. There's no coming back from this shit! As far as I'm concerned, the relationship is over and so is the fucking wedding!" I huffed as I rested the phone against one of the couch pillows.

"Yeah... Damn, girl, I'm so sorry you had to go through all this and on your graduation night of all nights," she said, sucking her teeth and shaking her head.

"Do you know how many times I could've lost my virginity to anybody over the course of twenty-two fucking years, and I saved it for my marriage! For him!"

"Well, aren't you glad you didn't fuck him? It would've been way worse that it is right now, girl"

"Yeah, you're right about that. I just need to get the fuck out of here," I said as I looked around the apartment.

"Where would you even go?" she asked.

"I don't know... My parents bought me two tickets to Miami as a graduation present for four days. Derrick and I were supposed to go, but I'm thinking about turning it into a girl's trip. What do you think?" I asked as I picked up the phone again.

"I think that's an amazing idea. You know I'm down. When?"

"I think we would have to leave within the next week or so. I'll have to check."

"Who all would we invite?" she asked.

"Um... you, me, Shante, and Megan."

"Hmmm... I don't know about Megan," she said, shaking her head at the screen.

"Why not? What did she do?" I asked, trying to get the tea.

"That bitch be moving shady, and I don't wanna have to drown her ass in the ocean while we down there." She chuckled.

I laughed along with her and shook my head.

"Thanks for the laugh, girl."

"You my girl. You know I got you with the jokes, but um, back to this trip..."

"Fine. How about just you, me, and Shante then?"

"Sounds like a plan. I'll hit up Shante tonight and let you know what she says."

"Okay, girl. Thanks."

"I love you, Raqi. Everything is going to be okay, okay? We gon' turn up so damn hard in Miami that the knob will break! And who knows? You may be able to find you a little Miami spring fling down in the 305 to really take your mind off that fuckboy Derrick!"

"Um, you're banned from speaking his name ever again."

"Say no more. I'll just refer to him as 'that bitch,'" she said as she put her fingers in air quotes.

"That's better."

"Yeah, girl. I already got it down pact, listen. You talk to that bitch today? Did that bitch apologize yet? I hope that bitch gets hit by a bus!" She laughed.

I laughed again and shook my head.

"Wishful thinking, but we'll see. And thanks again for the laugh. I love your crazy ass, too."

I hung up the phone and sighed then walked down the hallway to my room. I flipped on the lights and looked around. Derrick's stuff was still laid up in the corner. There were pictures of us all over my walls and in picture frames around my room. I never knew what it felt like to be a woman scorned until that moment. As much as I wanted to have an Angela Bassett moment with "Not Gon' Cry" playing in the background, I didn't want to risk setting my entire apartment on fire with all of my belongings in it. It was the first time I'd ever gotten my heart ripped out of my chest, stepped on, and left for dead.

Derrick was all I knew. He was all I ever wanted. I knew one thing was for sure. I never wanted to feel that type of pain ever again. Tears drained from my eyes in abundance as I jumped on top of my bed and started ripping the photos off the walls one by one, tossing them in my wire trashcan. Whatever clothes or electronic devices he had left went straight into the bathtub. I made my way into the kitchen, found the bleach underneath the kitchen sink, and headed back into the bathroom. I filled up the tub with water and then poured bleach all over his clothes, laptop, and red Beats by Dre headphones. I lifted the toilet seat and poured the contents of the ripped photos into the toilet.

"Good riddance, you stupid ass nigga," I mumbled as I spit on our pictures and then flushed the pieces down the toilet.

CHAPTER TWO

Raquel

Although I still wasn't in the mood to party or smile, Camille, Shante, and I boarded our flight to Miami a week later.

"How are you holding up?" Shante asked me as we hooked our seatbelts on the plane.

"Eh, I don't know." I shrugged. "Just hanging in there I guess."

"Has he tried to reach out to you?"

"Every day."

"What exactly did he have to say?" Camille asked, snaking her neck and rolling her eyes.

"Yeah, I mean, you caught him in the act. What else is there for him to say except for he's sorry?" Shante added.

"Yeah, I know." I nodded.

"Hold up! You're not thinking about taking him back are you?" Camille asked with an attitude in her voice.

"No... no. I'm not," I said, shaking my head.

"Good. Because if you would've said yes, I would've slapped you. Hard, too."

"Me too." Shante nodded.

"I mean, y'all gotta cut me some slack. Derrick is all I've ever known. He was my first kiss, my first date... he's even my first love, and if I would've walked down the aisle, he would've been the first and only man I would've ever given myself too. That's a hard pill to swallow overnight..."

"Correction. He *was* your first love, Raquel. There are plenty more fish in the sea." Camille interrupted me.

"Bitch, and we about to go to the beach, so we gon' make sure we find you a fish or two," Shante added.

I shrugged.

"Yeah, you're right."

"Lawd God! Let us pray," Camille said, placing the palm of her hand on my forehead. "Lord God in Heaven, puh-lease let Raquel find her a fine ass summer bae or freaky spring fling down in Miami so that she can get her mind off her ex fuckboy named Derrick... oops... I mean *that bitch* and his wayward dick!"

"Hallelujah!" Shante added while waving her hand in the air.

"Yes, Lord, we ask that this bae be so damn fine that Raquel's panties get wetter than the Atlantic Ocean! And if you see fit, Lord, please let him have at least two more fine ass friends for us in favor of our good deeds. In Jesus' name we pray. Amen!"

"Amen!" Shante shouted followed by laughter.

The three of us laughed and joked all the way to Miami. By the time we got there, I had a new outlook on life and even love. I told myself that I was going to be open and have as much fun as possible while we were there.

* * *

As soon as we checked into our hotel, we changed out of our bummy airport clothes and into our cute Miami-ready bathing suits to hit the rooftop pool.

"Damn, bitch. You were really hiding that body underneath

all those layers of clothes you were wearing back in school, huh?" Camille asked as she hip bumped me.

I smiled and shooed her off.

"Girl, I had to keep the niggas focused on the books and not the booty!"

"You two are a trip." Shante chuckled.

"No, seriously though, Raquel, please tell me you brought clothes that will accentuate that booty and that flat stomach of yours while we're here."

"I brought... stuff." I shrugged.

"*Stuff?* What the hell is *stuff*?" Camille asked.

"Yeah, what in the hell does that mean?" Shante peered at me curiously.

"It means I brought dresses and heels."

"How high are the heels?" Shante asked.

"Yeah, because if you say anything under four inches, I'm going to drown you in the pool." Camille nodded.

"Maybe we should hit the mall just in case..." I told them.

"See? That right there tells me that you aren't ready for this trip. I told your ass to pack toothpaste, a toothbrush, string biki- nis, and condoms. You ain't listen!" Camille told me.

"A string bikini though?" Shante asked as she fell back against the beach chair laughing.

"Yes, bitch, a string bikini! I'm trying to have my girl fucked right out here so she can leave her virginity right here in the 305."

"I don't wanna lose my virginity to just anybody, Camille. You know I'm not like that," I said, shaking my head.

Camille sighed and slapped my thigh.

"Damn you and your good ass morals!"

"How about we just focus on catching some rays, some fine ass niggas, and no damn STDs!" Shante said.

"Sounds like a plan." Camille nodded.

While Camille and Shante spent their time posting pictures on Instagram and Snapchat, I laid on my beach chair with my nose all in Derrick's social media like the female Inspector Gadget

I was. I checked his latest Instagram posts, Snapchat story, Facebook posts, and his Twitter feed. There were still pictures up of the two of us on his Instagram and Facebook. His pictures were still on mine too. I sighed and wiped my eyes then placed my sunglasses on.

"Um, what are you doing?" Camille asked, peering over her designer sunglasses at me.

"Nothing... It's nothing," I said as I locked my phone and put it beside me.

"What were you looking at, Raqi?"

"It's nothing."

"Shante, come over here, girl. It's time for another damn intervention," Camille said, waving Shante over.

The two of them sat on the end of my beach chair and stared at me.

"What?" I asked.

Camille sighed and grabbed my right hand.

"Raquel Valentine, as your best friend, it is my civic duty to break you out of any funk that you may be in. I took this pledge in the first grade when we met, and I will not let you down, okay?"

"Okay." I nodded.

"Now, spill it. What's going on in that head of yours?"

I sighed and shook my head.

"I don't know. As much as I want to get over him, and I know that I should, it's hard. It's hard as shit. Yeah, I know he did me wrong, and I know he doesn't deserve me, but that doesn't change the way I feel about him in my heart."

"So what would make you happy right now?"

I shrugged my shoulders and wiped my eyes again.

"I don't know. It's like I don't know anything anymore. I'm just walking around and breathing because I know I have to. But it's like my body is on autopilot. My heart has checked out and so has my fucking brain."

"I've got a question," Shante interjected. "What'd you do with the ring?"

"I haven't done anything with it yet. That's the only thing I kept. I was thinking about mailing it back to him."

"Mailing it back! Hell no! Say it with me, Raquel. Pawn! P—A—W—N!" Camille spelled out the word.

"I second that," Shante nodded.

"Before you give me some witty rebuttal, hear me out. Would you rather sit here and sulk or at least pretend that you're having a good time to show his ass you aren't worried about him or that trick ass bitch, Yasmine?" Camille asked.

"Yeah, Raquel. Do it for the gram," Shante added. "Trust me. If you post that body of yours, you're going to get all the fish. Who knows? It may even take your mind off all of this and really make you smile." She shrugged.

"You're right." I nodded. "The way I'm feeling can't be healthy. I've got to do something to get myself out of this sour ass mood."

"That's the spirit! Now, get up and let me work my professional iPhone photography skills and get you a good picture." Camille held her hand out for my phone as I handed it to her.

I stood up and took a few photos to oblige my friends and let them post them for me along with some ratchet ass captions.

"Happy now?" I asked as I wrapped my cover-up around me and sat back down in my beach chair.

"Ecstatic." Camille smiled.

I shook my head and smiled. I was thankful to have friends like Camille and Shante who wanted to do everything in their power to pull me out of the heartbreak hotel I had been living in for the past week or so. Camille and I had been best friends since the first grade. Shante joined the crew in middle school. The three of us used to call ourselves a mix between Destiny's Child and 3LW.

After graduating high school, the three of us went in different directions for the first time. I attended Alabama State University and studied mass communications and business management, while Shante attended Georgia Tech on a full scholarship. Camille stayed behind in our hometown of Charleston, South Carolina and took a few classes at our local community college. Our Miami trip was the first time the three amigos had been together since Shante and I had Christmas break.

"So, what are we doing tonight?" I asked, trying to put my best foot forward.

"I heard Club LIV is poppin'," Camille said.

"Okay. Well, let's try there then."

"But first... the mall," Shante reminded us.

Later That Night...

I found myself wearing a dress that barely covered my unmentionables and trying to keep my balance in four-inch heels.

"You're standing like a baby deer," Shante told me.

"Ol' Bambi lookin' ass," Camille joked as she threw a shot back.

"Fuck both of y'all!"

Camille laughed and swatted my arm.

"Come take this shot, Raquel. It'll loosen your stiff ass up."

"Fine. What is it anyway?" I asked seconds before tossing it down the back of my throat.

"Vodka."

I coughed a bit and held my chest as the burning sensation dissipated.

"What the hell! This is not vodka!"

Camille laughed and shook her head.

"Did I say vodka? I meant Ever Clear, girl."

"I hate you! I think I'm drunk already just off of one shot!"

"Good. Let's go!"

Camille and Shante locked arms with me, and we walked down the hallway to the elevator.

"Everybody got their IDs?" I asked before pressing the button.

"Yes, mama bear. Now, press the button so we can go twerk on some bitches' boyfriends!" Shante told me as she hip bumped me and laughed.

"Yeah. I'm ready to shake my ass tonight!" Camille added.

When we arrived at the club, it was live. There were people dancing and the drinks were flowing everywhere. I could feel the sweat in the air as I wiped my brow. My heels clacked behind Camille and Shante's as I followed them straight to the bar. Camille ordered two rounds of shots for us and then we headed to the dance floor. We were immediately swept up by random men asking for individual twerk sessions.

"What's your name?" the guy I was dancing with asked in my ear.

I shook my head from left to right, ignoring him, and continued to dance. I didn't want to get to know anybody. I just wanted to let loose and dance.

"I said what's your name, sweetheart?" he asked again.

Instead of turning him down, I turned my head to look back at him and was pleasantly surprised. He looked to be over six feet tall. He had milk-chocolate skin, long dreadlocks that were freshly done and a blinding white smile.

"Raquel," I said as I leaned my head back on his chest.

"That's a beautiful name for a beautiful woman, Raquel. I'm Dallas Price. Where are you from?"

"How do you know I'm not from here?" I asked.

"I'm ashamed to say I come here quite a lot, and I've never seen anyone as beautiful as you here *ever*, and I've lived in the 305 all my life."

I smiled.

"Does that line work with all the girls?" I asked, writing him off as just another player in my head.

"I wouldn't know. I've never said it to any other girl before."

"Somehow, I find that hard to believe."

13

"And why is that?"

"I mean, look at you. You're a very... *very* nice looking man. You have an Ace of Spades bottle in your hand and don't think I didn't notice that blinging ass chain around your neck."

"So I see aside from being an amazing dancer, you're also an observant woman. I like that in my women." He smiled.

"In your women, huh? Who said I was interested in joining your entourage of women?"

"You're not, but you seem like the type that could be my woman—Singular."

Feeling a bit flirty, I continued to play along.

"I think you skipped the part where you ask for my number." I smirked.

"And she's witty, too. I'm liking you more and more, Miss Raquel."

"Trust me. It's all this liquid courage pouring out of me. I'm really not this talkative with strangers," I admitted.

"Well, I tell you what. You go ahead and put your number in my phone, and then I'll call you. That way we won't have to be strangers to each other for too much longer," he said as he handed me his black iPhone.

I put my number in his phone and saved it.

"Here you go," I said, handing it back to him.

"You didn't just give me a fake number did you, Raquel? I don't have time to be walking out of here with my heart broken tonight. I've got an image to uphold."

"I guess you'll just have to call it and see."

Dallas eyed me closely and then pressed the call button. A smile made its way across his face when he saw my phone light up in my hand.

"Now, would you look at that?" I joked.

"That's what's up, sweetheart. I'm going to definitely hit you up, but I'm going to let you get back to having a good time with your girls," he said as he wrapped his arms around my waist and kissed my cheek. "You enjoy the rest of your night."

Dallas didn't get two steps away before Shante and Camille swarmed around me wanting all the tea.

"Damn, bitch. He was fine as fuck!" Camille said as she smacked my butt.

"Hell yeah!" Shante added. "Now, spill it. What's his name? What's he do? Is he married? How many kids he got?"

"Slow your roll, girl. I didn't get all that information!"

"It seemed like y'all was over here exchanging everything but social security numbers the way y'all were rappin' each other up!" Camille joked.

"Shut up! We didn't even talk that long!"

"Mmhm. Well, at least you two exchanged numbers, right?" she asked.

"Yeah, we did," I nodded.

"Yasssssss! Maybe you can get some Miami dick before we leave here after all! Lord knows I'm trying to!" Shante announced.

"Okay!" Camille said, giving her a high five.

"Y'all hos are a trip! C'mon. Let's go dance some more."

* * *

I danced for the rest of the night until I couldn't feel my toes anymore. By the time it hit 2:30 a.m., my head was spinning and I knew I had exceeded my alcohol limit. All I wanted to do was lay down, but Camille and Shante looked like they didn't plan to stop any time soon.

"Hey. I'm going to head back to the room, okay?" I yelled in Camille's direction.

"Huh?" she yelled back over the music.

"I said I'm going to head back to the room. I want to lay down."

"You want us to come with you?" she asked.

"No, no," I said, shaking my head. "I don't want to be a party pooper. You two stay here. I'll be fine."

"I don't want you to go alone."

"I'm a big girl. I'll be fine. The hotel is right down the street," I assured her.

"Fine, but text me as soon as you get there, okay? Shante and I will probably stay for another hour or so, and we'll be there."

"Okay. Have fun!" I said as I hugged her and Shante and then turned to leave.

I exited the club and walked down the block to the hotel. As soon as I walked through the doors, I pulled my phone out of my clutch and texted Camille.

> Raquel 2:47 a.m.: I made it to the hotel safe. Have fun and be safe.

> Camille 2:49 a.m.: Roger that.

My shoes clacked like a Clydesdale against the marble floor in the lobby as I made my way over to the elevator. I pressed the button for the eleventh floor and waited for the doors to close before resting my body against the back railing and peeling my aching feet out of my heels from hell. I could've slapped Shante and Camille for talking me into buying those four-inch stilettos from the mall. I rolled my eyes and groaned when the elevator stopped on the eighth floor. All I wanted to do was get down to my room and pass out. I pulled out my phone to see all the likes I'd gotten on the photos Camille and Shante had posted on my Instagram. When the doors opened, there was a man lying on the floor, bleeding from his mouth with his hand outstretched.

"Please... please, help me," he begged.

I screamed as I stood in between both doors. I hurriedly exited out of the app to call 911, but accidently hit the capture button. In the blink of an eye, the flash went off just when another man ran up and put two bullets in the begging man's chest. I screamed again and stepped back to press the elevator close buttons to escape.

"Oh my God! Fuck! Fuck! Shit!" I screamed as I fumbled with my phone.

I dropped my phone and my heels simultaneously and only bent down to pick up the phone. My hands were shaking as if I was standing naked in freezing weather. When the elevator hit the bottom floor, I screamed and ran out of the hotel with blood splattered all over the front of my legs and dress.

"Help! Help! There's a man! He's dead!" I screamed to anyone who would listen.

Everyone in the lobby stopped and stared at me. Nobody bothered to help, blink, or even move. When the elevator dinged again, all I heard were gunshots ringing through the air. I screamed again and bolted out of the hotel entrance, heading for any safe haven I could find. I ran down the street and down the side alley to stop and catch my breath. When I was sure there was nobody around, I held my phone in my trembling hands and dialed 911.

"What's your emergency?" the dispatcher asked.

"Hello, this is... this is Raquel Valentine and I just witnessed a..."

Before I could finish my sentence, there was a bag thrown over my head and everything went black.

CHAPTER THREE

Raquel

I woke up in the back of a moving vehicle that felt like it was driving much faster than whatever the posted speed limit was. My head was pounding as if I'd hit my head, and everything was still dark. I tried to move my hands, but they were bound at my wrists. I tried to move my feet next, but my ankles had been tied together as well. I could feel myself starting to panic and started to scream aloud.

"Help! Heeelllppp!" I screamed.

"Goddammit. Why didn't you tape the bitch's mouth shut?" a male said.

"Help! I can't breathe! Somebody help me! Please!" I yelled.

"Shut the fuck up!" a male with a different voice shouted and kicked me in my back.

I winced in pain and started crying.

"Pl—please just tell me what you want from me. I don't know anything. I didn't do anything!" I said, trying to plead for my life.

"You tell that to the boss," the first male said.

"We're here," the other one announced.

The vehicle abruptly stopped, and my body rolled without

my permission. I heard the back doors open and then was grabbed roughly and thrown over someone's shoulder. I could feel all the blood rushing to flood my brain on top of already being drunk.

"I think I'm going to be sick," I muttered before throwing up inside the bag that was on my head.

"What the fuck!" the male yelled and dropped my body on the ground.

I groaned in pain and laid there unable to move any of my limbs.

"Yo, take the bag off her head." I heard a new male's voice.

"But what about?"

"Just do it," he said.

I heard the flick of a knife before they cut the dark, smelly bag from around my head. When the bag dropped from around my face, I inhaled deeply and then coughed, causing me to throw up once more.

"What the fuck is up with this bitch?" the new male said. "Law is not going to be happy about this. Get her cleaned up then bring her in."

The male who dropped me scooped me up by my arms and dragged me to what looked like the back of a cargo van. He took a few paper towels to wipe my face and splashed some bottled water on my face.

"Let's go," he said as he pulled me up by my arms, placed a new bag over my head, and tossed me back over his shoulder like a rag doll.

I could feel the drafty air riding up my short dress as he carried me. Since I couldn't see, I relied on my other senses to help me. There were at least four different but deep voices talking around me. I heard the squeaking sounds of rodents nearby, which instantly made my body tense up, guns cocking in the distance, and feet shuffling against hard flooring. I could smell stale water around me as mosquitos feasted on my sweet skin.

The men were talking around me, mumbling about the dress

I had on, the length of my legs, and how smooth my skin looked. I was repulsed. My adrenaline was pumping strong. I had never been more terrified in my life. *Calm down, Raquel,* I kept repeating inside my head like a mantra. I didn't want them to see me losing my shit, but I couldn't pull myself together to save my life.

I winced in pain when my body slammed down onto a hard surface. I sat there, crying as silently as I could. Suddenly, the bag was ripped off my head. I gasped for air and slowly looked around, trying to take in as much of my surroundings as possible, but the room was slightly spinning. There was an oversized cockroach laying on his back beside my foot, trying to roll over. I jumped. There was barely any light in the room. It was still the wee hours of the morning. I looked down at myself, trying to quickly scan my body for any physical harm. Aside from the heart attack I felt like I was having, I was fine. My wrists and ankles were bound together with a zip tie, so I knew I couldn't run. I looked around at the four men as they silently stood around me as if they were a pack of wolves and I was their prey.

"Wh—where am I?" I asked as my lip trembled.

"You in the trap," one of them told me.

He was about five foot nine, stocky, and had a permanent mean mug on his face.

"W—what do you want from me? Is it... is it money? I don't have any money."

"You can't pay your way out of this one," another one told me.

I closed my eyes and tried to calm down. I prayed. I counted backward from one thousand. I even tried to think positive thoughts, but none of it worked.

"Please... please don't hurt me, I—I'll do whatever you want," I said, hesitantly.

"Whatever we want, huh?" another one said as he rubbed his dry, ashy hands together.

They sounded like sandpaper. I cringed at the thought of him even getting close to me or even touching me.

"That's enough," I heard another male voice yell from behind me.

He stepped so close to me that I could feel his cool breath against the nape of my neck. I shivered. I knew I shouldn't have turned around, but when I heard his voice, I couldn't help myself.

* * *

Ian

I was beyond pissed off when I heard the news that there was a witness to the murder I'd had my hittas commit. It was supposed to be a smooth in and out situation with only one casualty and definitely no one outside of us knowing what had happened. I had to crawl out of my bed, throw on some clothes, and make it down to one of my trap houses all because of somebody who seemed to be in the right place at the wrong time.

I expected the witness to be some pussy ass nigga or one of the people who worked at the hotel, but what I saw was different. I walked up behind her without seeing her face and whispered in her ear.

"Do you know why you're here?" I asked as I leaned down.

The girl slowly turned her head to the left and locked eyes with me. We both studied each other's faces for a few seconds in silence. I know she noticed all of the tattoo ink around my neck and hands despite the black hoodie I was wearing. She was beautiful, though, more beautiful than I expected her to be. She looked scared, which was a good thing. I was going to put the fear of God in her to let her know I was not the one to be fucked with.

"Do you know why you're here?" I asked again, snapping her out of her trance.

"N—no. No," she said, shaking her head.

She sniffed and tried to tilt her head back to try to keep the tears from falling.

"Where's her phone?" I asked my younger brother, Blaze. He was a younger and somewhat lighter version of myself.

"Right here, Law," he told me.

"Here," I said, handing the phone to her. "Unlock it."

"W—what?" she asked.

"I said fucking unlock it!" I yelled.

She took the phone from me and held it in her small, trembling hands. I watched her put in her four-digit code and then hand it back to me. I went straight to her camera roll, found the photo, and showed it to everyone, including her. I couldn't believe my eyes. I didn't know how she did it, but she somehow captured Blaze with the gun in his hand about to pop two bullets in a nigga's skull.

"Do you see this shit right here?" I yelled again.

She nodded repeatedly.

"Yes." She trembled.

"This is why you're here. You didn't see shit, and you don't know shit, you fuckin' hear me?"

"Yes. I got it. I understand. I won't say anything. I swear. Please, just let me go!" she begged.

I ignored her and continued to go through her phone.

"Fuck!" I yelled. "She called 911. They're probably tracking this shit right now!"

"What are we going to do with her fine ass?" one of my goons asked.

"You already know what has to happen to her. She's seen too much," another one added.

"Nah. Hold up a second. What's your name?" I asked her.

"R—Raquel."

"Who did you come here with?"

"M—my friends."

"Call them," I said, handing over her phone again.

"What?" she asked, looking me in the eyes.

"You heard me. Call them and let them know that you're good and everything is fine."

* * *

Raquel

I looked up at him and studied his face once more from the creases in his forehead down to his honey-brown eyes, his goatee, connected beard, and juicy lips. Then I nodded slowly and wiped my face, trying to get myself together before I called Camille. I knew she would be able to tell there was something wrong with me a mile away by just hearing the sound of my voice. If I wanted to live, I was going to have to lie to keep my life. I unlocked the phone once more, went to my call log, and tapped Camille's name.

"Put it on speaker," he told me.

I put the phone on speaker and waited for her to answer. A

part of me hoped she wouldn't. I wanted her to be passed out drunk and carefree. I didn't want to loop her or Shante into any of my shit.

"Raquel! Where the fuck have you been? It's been hours since we've seen you! We were worried sick!" Camille yelled as soon as she picked up the phone.

"I'm fine. Trust me!"

"Whereeee are youuuu?" she asked as her words slurred slightly.

"I uh... I'm fine."

"Yeah, but where are you? I thought you were coming straight back to the room, and yet, we're here and you're not, missy."

"I know... I um... I won't be flying back with you guys," I told her.

"Hold up. What do you mean you won't be flying back with us?"

"Yeah. Why not? What the hell is really going on, Raquel?" Shante yelled from the background.

"I—I met someone."

"Bitch, the nigga from the club?"

"Yeah... um... him. That's where I've been. Just kicking it with him. I'm going to stay a little longer and catch a flight back after a few more days."

"Are you having a *How Stella got Her Groove Back* moment? Wait... Is he around?" she whispered.

"Something like that," I said, cracking a slight smile.

"Okay then. I always say the best way to get over one man is to get under a new one, so I'm glad you're finally taking my advice for once!"

"Yeah. I guess I am." I shrugged.

"Have fun and be safe! Call me as soon as your plane lands, okay?"

"Yeah, and wrap it up!" Shante yelled.

"Okay. I will."

"Pinky promise?" Camille asked.

"Promise pinkies," I told her while wiping a tear from my eye.

Before I could hang up, my phone was snatched out of my hand, and the call was ended.

"You did good," he said and then dropped my phone on the ground and crushed it with his sho. "No more phone for you."

I swallowed hard.

"So what happens to me now?"

"What do you think should happen to you for sticking your nose where it didn't belong?"

"Please... just let me go. I swear to God I won't say anything to anyone! I didn't mean for any of this to happen!"

"Funny thing about that is I was taught to shoot the messenger too," he said, pulling a gun out from behind his back.

"W—why?" I trembled.

"If you're playing both sides of the fence you're just as dangerous as the niggas that don't fuck with me."

"Listen, you don't understand! I don't know anything about what's going on, okay? Nothing! I'm not even from around here! You just heard me tell my friends that I'm not taking a flight back with them!"

"And you expect me to just believe that?"

"Yes! Please! I'm just here on vacation with some friends. I didn't mean to start any trouble. I just want to go home!" I cried.

He stared at me for a few seconds in silence. He tucked his gun away and turned to his left.

"Take her to the house and get her cleaned up. We'll figure the rest of this shit out in the morning."

"What?" one of the goons asked.

"You heard what I said," he told them and walked out.

"I pray you know what you're doing with this broad for all our sakes."

"Wait! Please! Please just let me go! I swear I won't say anything! You have my word! Just let me leave!" I pleaded.

All my begging and pleading fell on deaf ears. The same disgusting bag was placed back over my head, and I was escorted back out to the van. I was forced to lie face down on the dirty floor as the van sped off. All I heard was the loud screeching of tires against the pavement. I tried to make mental notes of the turns to no avail. I was in a city I'd never been in, so turns wouldn't help me figure out where I was being taken. I laid there with my eyes closed and tried to focus on one thing—Surviving.

CHAPTER FOUR

Raquel

T he sunlight still hadn't started peeking through the night sky by the time the van came to a halt and I was pulled out. I felt the circulation coming back around my ankles when the zip tie was cut so that I could walk.

"Let's go," the man said as he pulled the bag off my head.

"W—where are you taking me?" I asked.

"Just walk," he said as he grabbed me by the arm and pulled me.

I was led up the stairs of a house larger than anything I'd ever seen before. It was almost like a palace. I stared in awe as I walked up closer to the large, sandstone home. There were two large palm trees on the east and west side of the house with columns that stretched over twenty feet high. It had two front facing balconies, a pool, fire pit, two turrets, and what looked like an attached four-car garage. I was for certain it probably came equipped with secret passageways, booby traps, and a mote. It was the kind of place most people dreamed of living in but could never actually afford to.

"Where are we?" I mumbled.

"Stop talking and just walk."

I pursed my lips and continued to be dragged into the home. When we got inside, my feet slid against the slick marble floor. I caught a glimpse of the foyer as we walked past a room full of people. I lowered my head.

"Why the fuck would you bring her through here while I'm having a party, Blaze?" a woman yelled.

I looked up at her. She looked to be about my height without the four-inch heels she had on. Her skin was cocoa brown, and she had the word diva written all over her face. Her makeup was highlighted and contoured just right. Her long eyelashes fluttered every time she blinked, and her lips were plump and glossy.

"I'm moving her now, Shiya. Chill out. Go back to whatever you were doing. I got this."

"Who the fuck are you anyway?" she asked, as she looked me up and down with a less than desirable look plastered across her face.

I looked at the man whose name I'd just learned was Blaze as he held me tightly by the arm, hoping he would interject with a response.

"I told you I'm handling it. Just go back to your guests," he said as he pulled me along.

* * *

Nashiya could be a hotheaded mothafucka sometimes. I guess that's why my brother loved her so much. Other than that, I didn't see what kept him so loyal to her ass. She was a ratchet who just happened to look classy on the outside. Law and I were raking in big money, and with the money came the bitches. I, for one, took the pussy as often as it was thrown my way.

I pulled the girl around the corner and into a dark room. I let go of her arm, quickly flipped on the lights, and then proceeded to pull her into the direction of the bathroom.

"Get in," I said, pointing to the Jacuzzi bathtub.

"What?" she asked.

Without repeating myself, I walked over and turned on the water. Once it was filled half way, I scooped her little ass up in my arms and put her in the tub, clothes on and all. She sat there, trembling as I pulled out a knife and cut the zip tie from around her wrists. She instinctively rubbed them. They were red and looked like they hurt more than a mothafucka.

"So your name is Blaze?" she asked.

"Aston, but everybody around here calls me Blaze," I told her.

"And Law... That's the boss' name, right?" she asked.

"Yeah." I nodded and chuckled a bit.

"Who is he to you?"

"He's my brother," I responded.

"And Shiya?"

"You're asking a lot of fucking questions." I sighed and rubbed my head.

"I'm sorry."

"She's Law's... fiancée."

"Is he going to kill me? I swear to God I don't know anything!" she said.

I could sense her ass about to start panicking all over again. I shook my head as I looked her up and down.

"I don't know." I shrugged. "Now, wash up. There's towels and washcloths right over there. I'll be right outside the door when you're done."

I closed the door behind me and leaned against it. Truth was, I had no idea what Law was going to do to her. It was the first time in my life that I'd ever seen him let anyone live. I just prayed his ass knew what he was doing. For the most part, my brother was level-headed. I guess that came with being the middle child. Our oldest brother Wolfe was the hot head and I, being the youngest, was the wild child. It had always been that way, even when we were growing up. Even though I was only twenty-four, I had calmed down a lot from my younger days. When I was a teenager, I used to get into all types of shit—breaking into cars, stealing, robbing niggas, and hustling drugs. I had no chill. It wasn't until Wolfe sat me down and really had a talk with me on some man-to-man shit, that I decided to change my ways. He told me if I wanted to be a heavyweight in the game, I needed to chill the fuck out if I wanted to live to see twenty-one.

Law and I both took a hit the night we found out Wolfe had been killed in cold blood. He was robbed and killed in a drug deal that went wrong. Niggas found him at the bottom of the stairs lying in a pool of his own blood and feces a little over a month ago, and niggas had been feelin' it ever since. That was no way for my brother to go out. The shit was a set up from the start if you asked me. All niggas did out in Miami was try to come up off another nigga's success.

After that, we immediately set out to rain down on anybody who had anything to do with it. Bodies were going to fall all over Miami, and we weren't going to show any fuckin' remorse for it either. Law was the next in command now that Wolfe was gone, and I was his right-hand man. So, without Law even asking anything of me, I got word of who killed my brother, and I handled it personally with two bullets straight to the nigga's chest. It just so happened to be one of our fucking rivals, Damien Price, the oldest of the Price brothers.

Our families had been going to war over drug territory and respect since my dad was running things back in the day. They were all just some jealous, pussy ass niggas in my eyes. Anytime we were in the same presence, shit felt cold and it was always on. Law and I both knew that we had to send a strong message and that message was that nobody was to ever fuck with the Calloway brothers again.

* * *

Raquel

I slowly sat up after he closed the door behind him and cried. I watched my tears drop one by one into the warm water as I sat there with my clothes still on. I was a fucking mess. After a few minutes of sulking and whimpering, I lifted my leg and stared at the bottom of my feet. They were black and looked disgusting. Water spilled out over the side of the tub as I undressed and threw my soaking wet dress onto the floor. I grabbed a washcloth and submerged it in the water. A million thoughts raced through my mind. I didn't know how much longer I'd have to stay alive. I didn't even know if I wanted to be alive. Staying positive and keeping a "survival" attitude was harder than it sounded. There was no light at the end of the tunnel as far as I was concerned.

I sat and watched the water slowly drain out of the large tub. When I was the only thing left inside it, I slowly stepped out and wrapped a towel around my body to start drying off. I felt like a human again for the first time in what felt like days. My hair was clean and free of chunks of throw up and so was my body. After I dried off, I noticed a bathrobe hanging on the back of the door. I walked over and put it on, dropping the towel to the ground beside my dress.

"Are you done?" Blaze asked as he knocked on the door simultaneously.

"Y—yeah," I replied as I wrapped my hand around the doorknob.

I turned the knob and pulled the door toward me. Blaze was standing on the other side, staring at me. I let my eyes scan him from top to bottom. He was about six feet tall with caramel skin. He had a low haircut with a few loose braids at the top, thick eyebrows, and a thin moustache with a little bit of chin hair. He resembled Law in many ways, except he had more of a baby face. He didn't have the matching goatee and beard like his brother did. There was a large tattoo on the right side of his neck that consisted of a green dollar sign, a roll of money, diamonds, and the words *God's Child* in the middle.

"Did that hurt?" I asked, pointing to his neck.

"Oh. I mean, no tattoo feels good, but as long as it looks good, that's all that matters to me," he said, flashing me a half-smile.

I admired how white and straight his teeth were. Just looking at them instinctively made me smile back.

"So uh... what now?" I asked as I pulled the robe tighter to my body. "I don't have any clothes."

"Oh shit... yeah... um... shit. Stay here. I'll be right back."

I watched Blaze scurry out of the room and close the door behind him. I shook my head. It was clear he didn't know what the hell he was doing. I opened the bathroom door wider and took in a panoramic view of the large gold and white bedroom.

The carpet was as white as snow and looked like people barely walked around on it. There was a large California king bed against the wall with a large, fancy gold headboard behind it. The white pillows looked as soft as clouds. There were gold curtains hanging from the twenty-foot high ceilings and a separate living room with a fireplace separating the two rooms in one. I walked over to the window and slid my hand down the thick curtain fabric. The crown molding around the walls was pure gold. I put both hands on the French door handles and pushed them open to step out on the balcony. The air was moist and warm. I let the slight breeze blow through my curly, wet hair. It was the first time I hadn't been afraid to close my eyes.

My thoughts were interrupted when I heard the bedroom door open. Blaze was back with company. I turned to walk back inside the room and was face to face with Law. He seemed to wear a permanent scowl every time he saw me. It was as if he hated the sight of me.

"Here," he said, handing me a pile of clothes. "See if you can fit these."

"Who do these belong to?" I asked as I took them from him.

"Do you want clothes or not?" he asked, answering my question with a question.

My forehead scrunched up as I looked at him. He acted like he was doing me a favor. All I wanted to do was go home. And to live... to live and go home. In that order.

"Thank you." I nodded.

I walked past him and headed back into the bathroom to change. I slid on the pair of Gucci sweatpants and t-shirt. I pulled the drawstring tight to fit my small waistline and opened the door.

"What is my role in all this?" I asked without looking up.

"Right now, you're just a liability that needs to be handled." I heard a female voice.

I immediately looked up and saw Shiya staring me up and down and Law walking up right behind her.

"Excuse me?" I said, ready to pop off.

"You heard me." Shiya snickered.

* * *

Law

"Nashiya, that's enough," I said, holding my hand up and looking over my right shoulder at her.

I knew if I hadn't stepped in when I did, Nashiya wouldn't have backed down. She was a pistol-popping, loud mouth, bougie ass girl from around the way. We had been together for five years, and I decided to propose to her almost three months ago. She was the Bonnie to my Clyde, but as beautiful as she was, I didn't know why she seemed to be so threatened by Raquel's presence. Nashiya was a ten in my eyes. She always kept her hygiene in tip-top shape, her body looked amazing in anything she wore, and most importantly, I knew she was down for a nigga come hell, high water, or bullets. The last part was all that really mattered to me, though.

Ever since I was young, I knew I was born to be different. My pops raised my brothers and I to be strong men who ain't take no shit from nobody. We all got started in hustling because that's how we were raised. Our father was the man back in the day. He always had money. I knew all of us wanted to be just like him in one way or another. Now, my father was a one-woman man unlike my brothers. Wolfe and Blaze were some straight up hos. As soon as we started raking in the big money, all they saw was green, and with the green came a smorgasbord of ass and titties. Don't get me wrong. I knew there was a sea of pussy waiting for me to swim in, but I was a one-woman type of man just like my pops.

"Um, hello? Law?" Nashiya said, snapping her fingers in my face.

She sucked her teeth and folded her arms across her chest. I looked over at Raquel, who glanced up at me with a grateful look on her face then quickly lowered her eyes. Blaze walked over and put a crumpled up McDonalds bag on the coffee table in front of her.

"Here," he told her.

"Eat," I demanded, cutting her off before she could respond to him.

"I don't... I'm not hungry," she said, clearing her throat.

I knew she was lying. She looked like she was starving. I had to give her credit, though. She was smart for not trusting anything we gave her. I walked over to the table, opened the bag to pull out a french fry, and bit it to show her we weren't trying to poison her.

"You're worth more to me alive, Raquel... For now. So, eat. When you're done, get some sleep. When the sun comes up in the next hour or so, I'll figure out what I'm going to do with you," I told her and then walked out.

* * *

35

I watched Blaze follow behind Law while I stayed behind. I walked over and stood across from Raquel on the other side of the table with my arms still folded. I was mad at him for trying to shut me down in front of her yellow ass.

"What's your name?" I asked with a smug look across my face.

"Raquel," she said as she slowly put a fry up to her dry ass lips.

"Well, Raquel, I'm Nashiya and I think there's something that you need to know. Law is my man, and I'm his woman, soon to be his wife," I said as I flashed my expensive ass diamond ring in her face. "So, don't even think about fucking crossing me, him, or anybody else in this fucking house. I'm the type of bitch that'll roll up on you anytime and anyplace guns blazing. Remember that. I don't play around when it comes to my man or my money, honey." I smirked.

I couldn't quite put my finger on it, but something inside of me hated the sight of Raquel from the moment I laid eyes on her, and I didn't even know her. I'd worked too damn hard and sacrificed too much to let some crybaby ass female with a cute little body and nice smile tear down the empire that I was about to marry into. I loved Law. I knew him like the back of my hand, so I knew he wasn't the type to stray away because he got a whiff of some new pussy. He knew better than that. But I knew her little ass was up to no good, and the quicker Law got her the fuck from around us the better. She looked like the type of bitch to run straight to the police and be on some snitch shit, and that was not respected around us. Raquel looked up at me and shook her head.

"What are you shaking your head at?" I asked.

"I promise you I don't want either, Nashiya. I just want to go home. That's all," she said.

"Good. Let's just make sure you keep it that way, and we won't have any problems," I told her as I turned my back to leave.

I sashayed away as her pathetic ass sat there and chewed another french fry. I was going to make it my business to have Law escort her fucking ass right off the property as soon as possible so that we could get back to our regularly scheduled lives, which consisted of him making boss moves and making money and me planning my dream wedding to my dream nigga. I didn't know why he chose to keep her ass alive in the first place. That wasn't like him, and that worried me. Law had always been level-headed and calm but would still wreak havoc among anyone who tried to step on his territory. My baby was a god in my eyes, a king even. I knew it the first time I met him. And if little Miss Raquel ever wanted to see her friends or family again, she better had played by our rules, or I would kill her weak ass myself.

CHAPTER FIVE

Raquel

I woke up without even realizing I'd fallen asleep and quietly lifted my body off the couch. I slid on the socks that lay on the floor beside me and walked over to the French doors. I quietly opened them. The humidity in the air was stifling. I looked over the balcony and shook my head. It was a long way down to the ground.

"Shit," I mumbled to myself, unaware of how in the hell I was going to make it out of there alive.

There was no way I could just walk out of the front door without being noticed. There was a man sitting on the other side of the bedroom door, waiting for me to get antsy so he could pop a bullet in me. I also knew I wasn't Catwoman and didn't know the first thing about scaling a building. I didn't have time to wait and see what Law's decision would be when the sun fully came up. I had to go. The only plan I had was to get out and run. I would make everything else up as I went along.

I rested my head in the palms of my hands as I leaned over the balcony. I didn't know what to do. *Think, Raquel. You're a smart girl. You can get through this. You can escape*, I told myself repeatedly. I walked back into the bedroom, quietly pacing the floor, and looked over at the bed. I ran over, pulled all of the sheets off the bed along with the fitted sheet, and tied them together like I'd seen on television. I ran back out to the balcony and looked over it again.

"Here goes nothing," I said as I tossed the rope made of bed sheets over the balcony, while tying the other end to the framing.

I threw one leg over the edge and held onto the sheets for dear life, inching down as carefully as possible. When I ran out of sheet to hold onto, I dropped four feet down to the ground and groaned. As soon as I stood to my feet, I took off running for my life without looking back. I felt free but still shook to my core.

"Stop her!" I heard someone yell behind me.

My legs went into overdrive. I ran so fast I could feel my lungs bleeding inside my chest, begging me to stop for air. When I got to the end of the road, I hastily made a left turn and ran some more. I could see the headlights behind me and heard engines revving, but I didn't stop. I couldn't. I ducked down into a low passage way and kept going. The plan was to get to civilization, anywhere where I could be around people and could call for help.

"Please! Please, help me!" I yelled to the first man I saw, walking.

"Excuse me?" he asked.

"Please, do you have a phone I can use? I've been kidnapped, and I know my kidnapper is looking for me! If you could just please let me use your phone to call for help, I'd appreciate it," I said, breathing heavily.

"Kidnapped, huh?" he asked.

"Yes." I nodded, getting more irritated and impatient by the minute. "Now can I please use your phone, sir?"

I felt stupid standing in front of a man who looked to be in his mid-to-late forties. He had on regular street clothes, a bald-head, and a tattoo of a snake on his neck. It didn't matter what he looked like though, using his phone was all I cared about.

"If I give you my phone, what will you give me in return?" he asked, running his tongue over his bottom set of grills.

"Excuse me?" I asked scrunching up my forehead.

I felt the man grab me with both hands. I let out one scream before another set of hands covered my mouth and proceeded to drag me into a nearby alleyway.

"You scream again, you fucking die," the bald man warned me.

I wriggled and resisted as much as I could to no avail. The one with his hands around my mouth removed his hands. I bit him as hard as I could, and I worked my feet free to kick the bald one in the jaw. He stumbled backward, and I tried to run away, but the bald man grabbed my foot. I tripped and felt him pulling at my ankles, trying to grab me. I screamed as he mounted me from behind and flipped me over. That's when I saw the knife he was wielding in his hand. My eyes widened and I gasped.

"Didn't I tell you if you screamed again you'd fucking die?" he said, holding the knife to my throat.

He put his dirty left hand over my mouth and proceeded to run the back of the sharp knife across my throat with his right hand.

"Say goodbye, princess."

I closed my eyes, giving up. I was scared out of my mind, and after all I'd been through, I was ready to die. There was no way I was getting out of that situation to make it home, and even if I did, I knew I'd always be looking over my shoulder. That was no way to live. My eyes popped open when I heard two gunshots ring off into the alley. I looked up and saw the bald-headed man with two bullet holes perfectly placed in the middle of his head. He fell off me and landed beside me. I screamed, scrambling backward, trying to get to my feet. I looked over my shoulder and saw Law standing there with his smoking gun pointed in the direction of the man whose hand I'd bitten.

* * *

Ian

"Hey, hey I don't want any problems," the man told me with his hands up in the air.

He looked and sounded like a scared little bitch. He slowly backed away three steps and then turned his back to haul ass. I glanced down at Raquel and then looked back up at the man running away and let my gun ring out two more times, piercing the coward right in his back. He was quick to try and rape a woman but wouldn't face a grown ass man. He deserved both bullets that I lodged into his body, maybe even more. I watched him fall to his knees and die right where he laid.

"Bitch ass nigga," I said as I slowly lowered my arm and then looked down at Raquel again who looked like she'd just seen her entire life flash before her eyes.

I didn't know why I spared her life twice in not even knowing her for whole twenty-four hours. She was nothing but a casualty, and I could've easily shot and killed her ass in that alley too and walked away with my life back in one piece. But I couldn't. There was something about her that I just couldn't shake. No one on Earth had ever made me feel that way before, not even Shiya. I didn't know if it was the innocent persona Raquel gave off anytime she was around me or how naive she was about the lifestyle she'd fallen into. Whatever it was, it wouldn't let me harm a hair on her body, and I wasn't going to let anybody else bring harm to her either. I just had to figure out what I was going to do with her.

CHAPTER SIX

Raquel

I couldn't take my eyes off Law. The way he looked at me... there was so much fire in his eyes. I saw the savage inside him. His eyes were cold and empty. He didn't fear anything. I was astounded. The man who kidnapped me had just saved my life. That's when I learned that not all monsters were scary.

"Get up. We gotta go now," Law said.

I sat there, still unable to take my eyes off him and still unable to move like my entire body had been cemented to the pavement underneath me. Before I could get another word out, Law scooped me up in his arms and carried me to a black SUV. He put me in the passenger seat and strapped my seatbelt across my body. He got in the driver's seat and sped off down the road.

My body was slumped against the door. I felt disgusting. My mind was spinning. I wanted to scream, cry, fight, kill, and throw up all at the exact same time. I could still feel both of their hands around me and could smell everything from their breath to the dried ketchup under their fingernails. All I could think about was washing their strong, disgusting scents off my body.

"Did those niggas fucking touch you?" he asked, looking over at me.

The vein in the middle of his forehead and the one in his neck bulged out. I looked down at my shirt that was ripped at the shoulder. I also had a few cuts on my arms from struggling to get away. Other than that, I was fine *physically*.

"If you hadn't showed up when you did, I don't know what would've happened," I admitted as I wiped a tear from the corner of my eye.

"Look, you don't have to talk about it. Let me just get you back in the house so you can get yourself cleaned up."

When Law stopped at a red light, I glanced over at him. He really was a gorgeous, brave man. It was the first time since I'd been in his presence that I'd actually saw him as a human being. I could see why Nashiya was so protective of him. If he did what he did for me after only knowing me for less than twenty-four hours, I couldn't imagine what lengths he would go through to protect the woman he intended to make his wife.

"Thank you," I said reluctantly.

"For what?" he asked, taking his eyes off the road to look at me.

"For... you know... what you did back there. You saved my life, Law"

"You're more trouble than you're worth, you know? I knew that from the moment I laid eyes on your little ass."

My forehead scrunched up. I simply thought he was going to say thank you, but his response was far from that.

"Then why not let me go? Why chase me? Why go through all the trouble to save me or spare my life again?" I asked as I straightened up my posture in the passenger seat.

"There's more to all of this than what you think you know."

"Like what?"

"None of which concerns you right now," he said.

"It has to. If not, I wouldn't be here, right?"

Law let out a loud sigh and shook his head.

"The shit you saw at the hotel that night. The man who was killed... he deserved it."

"What does anyone do to be killed in cold blood like that?"

"He killed my older brother, Asaad, or Wolfe as the streets called him."

I lowered my head, feeling bad for speaking out of turn.

"I'm sorry about that. Do you know why?"

"Niggas don't have to have a reason to kill you nowadays, especially not out here in the streets. Shit, I grew up around street niggas. Been around them all my life, and if it's anything I learned, it's that the streets don't love you. Shit just happens in the streets that take you away from the people that do."

Even though I didn't know much about the streets other than what I'd seen in movies or documentaries on TV or Netflix, I knew he was speaking the truth. I glanced out of the windshield and noticed we were pulling back up to the house.

"You can walk this time?" he asked.

I nodded without speaking, eager to douse myself in soap and water.

"Good. Head up and take a shower. I'll be in to check on you in a few."

"Okay," I nodded.

"Oh, and Raquel, don't ever make me fucking chase you like that again."

"I won't."

I got out of the car and didn't stop walking until I was in the bathroom with the door closed and locked behind me. I made my way over to the shower and turned it on to let the water heat up. I stood in front of the mirror and slowly got undressed. I noticed there were bruises on my arms and around my neck along with the cuts I'd already noticed. I continued to undress and then got in the shower. Even the slightest touch of the water seemed to hurt my sensitive skin. I groaned a little but made sure to scrub through the pain.

When I stepped out of the shower, I wrapped a fresh towel

around me and let the steam flood out of the bathroom into the cool bedroom. I didn't even bother redressing; I just climbed in the large bed with the damp towel wrapped around my body. All I wanted to do was forget anything that had transpired in my life in the past twenty-four hours. A part of me hoped that it was all just one big ass nightmare and that when I woke up, I would be back in my apartment or at least in my hotel room with my friends and everything would be normal again.

As soon as I closed my eyes, there was a knock on the door. I knew it had to be Law. I flipped on the lamp beside the bed.

"Come in," I said.

* * *

Law

I walked into the guest room where Raquel was staying and watched her sit up in the bed while she pulled the bath towel closer to her body.

"Are you okay?"

"I guess." She shrugged.

"Okay. Well uh, just let me, Blaze, or somebody around here know if you need anything. I'll let you get some rest."

"Wait!" she said, outstretching her arm to me. "I think I'm a little thirsty."

"You want water or something?" I asked.

"You got anything stronger than that?"

I smirked a bit and then nodded. I made my way over to the other side of the room and poured a shot of Hennessy in two glasses then headed back over to her. I sat on the edge of the bed and then handed one glass to her.

"What is it?" she asked, swirling the liquid around in her glass.

"Hennessy. Trust me. It'll take the bite out of the night, and it'll help you sleep better."

I took a sip first and then she followed suit. The cognac immediately burned my throat and every other body part on the way down, but I liked the feeling.

"Shit! I forgot how strong that shit was," she said, coughing a bit.

"It's not for the faint at heart. I'll say that."

"I do want to thank you again, though... for doing what you did for me."

"It's fine. I can't have you gettin' killed and shit, and I don't even know what I'm going to do with you yet."

"About that...you told me that the guy... that... what I saw happened because he killed your brother. I get that now, and I wouldn't go to the police about that. You destroyed the evidence, right? I mean, if I could erase the shit from my brain, I would. I swear I would, but I won't tell anybody. I promise you, Law. I won't."

"Who are you to me, Raquel?" I asked.

Although the shit she was saying sounded sincere, I didn't know who I could trust. All I wanted to do was protect my family, and I wasn't going to let anyone get in the way of that.

"What?"

"Who are you to me that I would just so easily take your word for it?" I asked, explaining myself.

"You know what? Doing whatever it is you're doing that got you this nice ass house and shit has done nothing but make you paid and paranoid," she told me.

I chuckled a bit because I knew she was right. I had been paranoid for a long time, damn near all my life. I'd just learned how to control it. Being paranoid wasn't always a bad thing. It kept me on my toes and always observing the people around me.

"Maybe you're right, but this hustlin' shit pumps through my veins. It always has. It's just a Calloway thing. You wouldn't understand."

"What do you mean?" she asked.

I sighed and set my empty glass down on the edge of the nightstand. I didn't know what it was, but the more I talked to her, the more I could tell she was genuine. That alone made me feel like I could talk to her about almost anything.

"I was eleven when my brother showed me our father's gun for the first time. It was me, him, and Blaze. He was only around eight at the time. The three of us were home alone. It didn't happen often, but since Wolfe was fourteen, pops thought he could handle being the man of the house for a few hours, you know? Mom was working, and our father was out running plays in the streets, doing his thing. Anyway, Wolfe called me into our room one day and said he had something he wanted to show me. Me thinking it was nothing, I stood and watched him as he reached underneath the bed and pulled out an old shobox. He put the box on the bed, looked over his shoulder at me, and then lifted the top to pull out a gun. That's when Blaze came running in. I guess it scared him because he pointed the gun right in Blaze's direction. All I remember was seeing a flash of silver in the air. He was so quick to pull the trigger. I didn't stand a chance at stopping him. Luckily, he missed Blaze but not by much. That was probably the scariest moment of my life. Goddamn, I was so fucking scared. The three of us stood there in silence. My ears were ringing like crazy. I had never heard a gunshot that close before. That's when Blaze started crying. Wolfe shoved the gun back in the box, and we both ran over to Blaze. We just kept telling him it was okay and that it was an accident, but he just wouldn't stop crying. I don't know...

I guess something about Blaze's screaming just did something

48

to Wolfe because he went back to that box, grabbed that old fucking gun, and pointed it at Blaze for a second time. I asked him what he was doing, you know? That was our baby brother and the way he looked at him... It scared the shit out of me. I yelled at him, tried to reason with him. All Blaze could do was scream. Wolfe just kept yelling, *'Shut him up before I do! I swear to God!'* I didn't know what to do. I couldn't think. I put my hand over Blaze's mouth and put my other hand over his eyes. His whole body was shaking and so was mine. I just kept whispering in his ear and begging him to be quiet.

Once he settled down, Wolfe lowered the gun. *'Don't you fucking tell on me,'* he told us. Blaze and I both nodded out of fear. That fear we had of Wolfe that young stuck with us for a long time. It resonated off of everybody who ever came within a foot of him. He fed off it. Our father was the same way."

"So what happened after that? Did you tell?" she asked me.

"Blaze did. Not right away... maybe a few weeks later. Mom kept asking what happened, and one day, he just spilled everything and started crying all over again. I'd never seen my father so angry before, at least not at us. He was probably scared, too, because we were all so young, and we were family, brothers. That's when he sat us all down and told us about the streets, guns, drugs, and everything in between. He emphasized the importance of the bond between a family, especially brothers. The last thing he said when he looked at us was *'What don't break a nigga, make a nigga,'* and it never came up again."

Raquel

Hearing Law's story had me at a loss for words. I almost wanted to cry. The way he told his story made me feel like I was right there in the room when everything happened. He was brave, handsome, and loyal wrapped up in one man.

"Wow," I said, shaking my head. "I can't even imagine."

Law looked at me out of the corner of his eye.

"It's not for you to understand. It's not for anyone to understand. I still think about it sometimes when I'm alone and I can finally get a moment to myself. I still see the gun and the look in Wolfe's eyes. I can picture him pulling the trigger like it was just a water gun or a BB gun even. An effortless kill, you know? My little brother could've been dead... That's why I'm so protective of him now. I vowed back then that I would never let any harm come to him. I take that I'm my brother's keeper shit for real," he said as his voice trailed off.

"I have a question."

"I might have an answer," he said, adjusting himself on the side of the bed.

"Who are you, Law?"

"You know enough about who I am."

"Yeah, but who are you really? I have a feeling that the man behind all this power is a different type of guy."

Law looked at me and shook his head as if to say to be continued. I could see it in his eyes how tired he was. Both of our eyes were getting heavier by the second.

"That's enough story time for tonight. It's gotta be damn near seven in the morning or somethin'. Get some rest, aight? Goodnight, Raquel."

"Goodnight, Law..."

I smiled at the way his voice cracked when he told me goodnight. Law lifted his body from my bedside after a few seconds of staring at me in silence and headed for the door. It was the first time I'd ever seen him look at peace or at least relaxed. It was evident that Law was a beautifully created human being from the top of his head to the soles of his feet. His facial features were designed by perfectionists. The way his abs contracted when he breathed was hypnotizing. A part of me wanted to lick his smooth, caramel skin. It looked sweet and inviting. I wanted to feel his arms wrapped around me again. I wanted him to take control of me. That's when it hit me. I didn't know if I was experiencing a case of Stockholm Syndrome or what, but something inside me was starting to fall for him.

CHAPTER SEVEN

Nashiya

I sat and stared at the large rock of an engagement ring sitting pretty on my ring finger. I'd worked hard to be the only woman standing at Law's side, and I finally had the ring to prove it. Soon, I'd have the Calloway name on the end of mine. I was ecstatic. I fell in love with Law the first moment I met him.

It was five years ago. I was chilling with my sister and her home girl down on the strip, killing time before I had to go to work. I was twenty-three at the time. I had never been to college or anything fancy like that. Hell, I barely made it out of high school by the skin of my teeth. I could honestly say I had no ambition back then. Anyway, I'd landed a job as a waitress at a bar on the strip and was about to clock in in the next thirty minutes.

"Damn, I swear I don't want to go to work today, y'all." I groaned.

"Then don't. Plus, you know JW havin' that boat party tonight. You bests be callin' in sick if you wanna roll with us," my older sister Shayla told me.

Shayla had always been a bad influence on me. I just didn't care to acknowledge it at the time.

"You know what? I think I do feel a little headache coming on," I said, touching my forehead with the back of my hand.

"That's more like it," Shayla smirked.

"C'mon. Let's get out of here," I said as I hopped off the low wall I was sitting on.

As soon as we started walking, a fine ass nigga walked by. I swear it was like everything around me started going in slow motion like I was in the Matrix or something. He glanced back at me, and of course, I made eye contact with him. The second our eyes locked, my stomach started doing backflips. He looked like money, trouble, and one hell of a good time, which were three of my favorite things.

"Did you see that fine ass nigga?" Shayla said, breaking her neck almost as hard as I was.

"Hell yeah, I did," her friend added.

"Both of you hos need to back up, aight? I call dibs. That's my fuckin' husband right there," I stated boldly.

"Dibs? Bitch we are not in elementary school," Shayla reminded me.

"Besides, didn't you and Dallas just break up like a few weeks ago? Are you sure you're ready to date a new nigga?" her friend asked.

"Hey, the best way to get over one nigga is to get under a new one, and that one is looking oh so good to me. Hold my stuff, Shay. I'll be right back."

I handed my sister my purse and jogged down the opposite end of the street to catch up with my future husband. My sister and her friend were right. I had just gone through a bad breakup with my ex, Dallas. We'd been together since high school, but then he started being a fuckboy, a broke one at that! Before seeing that fine guy, I had no interest in dating or even flirting with anybody with a dick swinging between their legs, but one sight of him had definitely changed my mind. My nose, eyes, and legs were wide open.

"Excuse me," I said, tapping him on the shoulder. "Don't I know you?"

"Nah, I'm sure you don't," he said, turning to look at me.

The way he looked at me made my heart stop. A voice inside my head screamed out, "Marry him, bitch!" From the moment he opened his mouth, I knew I wanted to be with him, and I would do anything for him.

"I'm sorry... My mistake. What's your name?" I asked.

"Law, and you?"

"Nashiya, but um... everybody calls me Shiya."

"Shiya, huh?" he asked.

"Yeah." I nodded.

"Well, here's the thing, Shiya. I'm not everybody."

My forehead scrunched up a bit, and I rested my hand on my hip. I couldn't believe he just tried to play me. Usually, I would've carried his ass all the way from Miami to China, but it was something about his demeanor that wouldn't even let me open my mouth to clap back. I had never seen a more handsome man. Just looking at him told me he was a boss. I swear, every time I looked at him, I felt tingles all over my body, especially in my panties.

"Okay then. Well, what do you want to call me, Law?"

"Mine," he said.

If I had been a cartoon character in that moment, my heart would've exploded out of my chest, my eyes would've popped out of my head in the shape of hearts, and the top of my head would've ejected straight up into the sky.

"A man who knows what he wants... I like that." I smiled.

"Put your number in my phone... Maybe we can hook up later or something."

"I'm supposed to be going to this boat party later tonight with my sister and her friend, but I'd rather chill with you," I told him with not an ounce of remorse in my body.

"Good." He smiled. "I'll be calling you later, Shiya."

The both of us turned to walk away at the same time, and I swear my legs were like Jell-O. I was in love. Later that night, Law stayed true to his word and hit me up. I'm pretty sure I answered on the first ring, because I was super pressed on his ass. He picked me up in a silver BMW and took me out to dinner. When he dropped me off, he kissed me, and if it had been the Fourth of July, there would've been fireworks taking off into the sky. His lips were so damn soft. I knew from that very moment that we had something special. I knew a man who carried himself the way Law did could have any woman he wanted, but that shit didn't scare me. I was a fighter back then, and I still am.

I would never let anyone know or show that the real reason I had a problem with Raquel was because she was so personable. She blew into our lives by chance, just like how Law and I met. Her basic ass was down to earth, and I think Law actually liked that about her. It didn't matter to me, though. I didn't care how cute she was or none of that. The bitch had to go. When I snapped out of my daze, I caught Blaze walking into the kitchen out of the corner of my eye.

"Hey, Blaze."

"Sup, Shiya."

"Question... How much do you know about this bitch Raquel?"

"Damn, Shiya. You still on that shit? I'm sure you already put the fear of God in that girl. Let it go."

"All I'm saying is it's been almost two weeks now. Her ass needs to go."

"What? You jealous or something?" Blaze asked, nudging me in the shoulder.

"Me? Jealous? Of that bitch? C'mon now. That's laughable. I just don't trust her. That's all."

"What did she do to you?"

"It's not what she did to me; it's what she could do to you or your brother. You're the one in that photo pulling that trigger, or did you forget?" I said, folding my arms across my chest.

"Yo, lower your fucking voice, aight? Besides, I had a mask on. She didn't see my face, and Law destroyed her phone the night it happened, so it's over. Boo. Poof. Bye bye evidence."

"Yeah, whatever," I said, sucking my teeth.

I watched Blaze fix himself a sandwich and walk back out of the kitchen as quickly as he'd entered. It was clear to me that he wasn't going to help me shoo her ass out of the house. I was the woman of the house, and before I was done with her, she was going to know that only one of us could be crowned queen, and it was most definitely going to be me.

* * *

Blaze

I made my way back up the stairs with my plate in hand when I saw Raquel walking down the hallway.

"Hey." She waved.

I gave her a head nod.

"What's up?"

"I wouldn't know. Just trying to kill time I guess." She shrugged.

"You about to go down to the kitchen or something?"

"I was thinking about it, why?"

"Shiya down there…"

"Oh ok." She nodded.

"Yo, what did you do to her ass?" I asked her, jokingly.

"What do you mean? I haven't done anything to her. We barely speak."

"Well, something you did got shorty down there pulling out her pink tracks over you. If I was you, I'd watch my back."

"That's all I've been doing since I got here. I'm still a pampered hostage around this bitch, remember?"

I didn't know if she was joking or being serious, but I laughed anyway. Raquel was charismatic in her own way. She was approachable, too. It also didn't hurt that she had a sexy ass body and beautiful face to match. Don't get me wrong. Nashiya was beautiful in her own way, too, but Raquel was all natural. She didn't have to wear expensive weaves or put on makeup before rolling out of the house. Her beauty was effortless. I knew that if I wasn't such a male whore, I'd shoot my shot with her. We would look damn good together, too.

"Yo, you real funny."

"Gotta laugh to keep from crying, ain't that what they say?" she said.

"Yeah, I guess."

"What type of sandwich is that?" she asked, staring at my plate.

"Turkey and cheese," I said as I took a bite. "It's good too."

I could tell she wanted a piece, but my ass was too hungry to share.

"Can I..."

"No," I said, cutting her off. "Bread, mayo, cheese, and turkey are downstairs."

"I was just going to ask for a bite." She pouted.

I rolled my eyes and exhaled deeply.

"Fine. You get one little ass piece, and you better break the shit off from the corner, too," I instructed.

"Thank you," she said, flashing a warm smile at me.

I watched her chew the piece of sandwich like it was a full course meal.

"Damn, you actually might be hungrier than me," I told her.

"Oh my gosh. It's like I don't know if I'm really that hungry or the sandwich is really that good. Either way, thank you."

"You're welcome," I said as I headed back down the hall towards my bedroom.

"Hey, Blaze," she said, stopping me.

"Yeah?"

"What are you about to do?"

I lifted my plate and looked at her as if to say *eat, duh.*

"Would you uh... care for some company?"

I eyed her for a second. I didn't know what kind of company she meant, but I was always down for whatever.

"You just want another bite of my sandwich, don't you?" I joked.

"Yeah, that too." She giggled.

Raquel followed me into my room and sat across from my bed on my black leather couch.

"So, what's up?" she asked as she let her hands fall into her lap.

"Nothing." I shrugged. "What's up with you?"

"Oh, you know... just waiting for the day your brother sees fit to ship me back home so I can act like none of this shit ever happened."

I snickered at her sarcasm and went about eating my sandwich. She stared at me with every bite I took like a dog waiting for scraps.

"Goddamn, girl. Here," I said, giving her the last bite of my sandwich.

"Thank you!"

"Yeah, yeah. Whatever."

"You know what it means when you give a woman the last bite of your food, right?" she asked mid chew.

"Nah, what?"

"That you love her." She laughed.

"Nah. I just got tired of you staring a hole in the side of my fuckin' face." I laughed.

I chuckled once more and shook my head, thinking.

"What?" she asked.

58

"It's nothing."

"Can't be nothing if it made you laugh again."

"It's just that shit you said sounded like something my mom would tell my pops back when we were growing up. That's all."

"I don't even know your mom and she already seems like the greatest woman on earth to me."

"She is. Ain't no other woman out here like her. That's for sure."

"I bet." She nodded.

"She and our father both taught us that the only thing the streets ever had to offer us was money, jail time, or death, but whenever we needed a way out, we always had family to fall back on. Family would always be there to show you a different kind of love than what you would get out in the streets, you know? Family is gon' love you no matter what."

"Wow. That's really deep." She nodded.

"Yeah, I know. I didn't really understand it until I got a little older. I used to be wild in the streets. Well, I'm still wild, but I was wilder. I was wild as fuck. I used to steal cars and rob niggas all for the hell of it. I used to just enjoy the thrill, you know?"

"And you were never afraid of getting shot or stabbed or anything like that?"

"I've been stabbed before," I said, showing her the scar on my shoulder.

"Wow. I probably would've fainted as soon as I saw the knife," she assured me.

"It was really just about making a name for myself though. Yeah, my last name carries weight, but I didn't want to be known as 'Baby Calloway' all my life."

"So... how'd you go from Baby to Blaze?" she asked.

"After that nigga stabbed me, I set his ass on fire."

"Wait. What?" she asked.

I chuckled a bit and shook my head.

"Yeah, I went to the gas station, put some gasoline in a cup, rolled up on his ass, and tossed it on him. Before he had a chance to react, I lit a match and threw it at his pussy ass."

"Wow," she said, sitting there with her mouth open. "I've never heard anything like that in my life."

"Yeah, you've definitely got to keep your eyes open out here, because the one time a nigga catches you slippin', you either off to jail or off to the morgue. I got lucky."

"You ever been shot at?" she asked.

"Of course. We used to hear gunshots outside of our house growing up so much that it never really phased us, you know? We were never really scared of guns. We knew what they could do when given the right motivation. They were always welcomed in our home until our father was killed."

"What happened to him, if you don't mind me asking?"

"Let the police tell it, he was killed in a random drive-by shooting. But we all know the truth. We know what really happened."

"What happened?" she asked.

"I shouldn't even be telling you this..."

"Who could I even repeat it to?" she asked.

I nodded my head. I knew she was right. Talking to Raquel was like talking to an empty vessel. I could just fill her up with all my thoughts and stories, and she'd have to keep them locked inside.

"He was shot in the chest during a fight. Our family has always had beef with another family out here in Miami."

"They sell drugs too?" she asked.

"Something like that."

"And the other family shot your father? Just like your brother, Wolfe?"

"How'd you know about my brother?" I asked.

"Law told me."

"What else did Law tell you?"

"Nothing. Nothing else."

"Mmhm," I said, not believing her.

"You ever think of stopping?" she asked.

"Stopping what? Hustlin'?"

"Yeah, that." She nodded.

"That's like me asking you if you ever thought of not breathing again. Why would you stop something that's kept you alive and well all your life?"

"You've got to want more though, right?"

"One thing about me is that I'm always thinking ahead, even though I'm young. Forever progressing, you know? I figure by the time I hit thirty, I'll have enough money set up to where I can fall back from the limelight and let some of these younger niggas on the come up and shine. I want to be remembered as an OG when I'm gone just like all the other men in my family."

"And what happens if you die before thirty? Then what?"

"Then I will have died a paid ass, respected ass nigga with the Calloway name. I'd rather die paid and respected than a broke ass nigga that nobody remembers any day of the week."

Raquel shook her head.

"You just can't leave it alone, huh?"

"Nah. I'm too addicted. I like living life fast and on the edge," I admitted with a satisfied smirk.

CHAPTER EIGHT

Lan

I was dressed and ready bright and early. I was meeting with Alistair Moreno, the biggest and oldest plug in Miami. I had only met with him a few times with Wolfe, never alone. I knew he was big on beautiful women and always had some eye candy around him, so I wanted to bring Shiya as a decoy just in case the feds were watching. I was the type of nigga to always play it more safe than sorry.

"Shiya, baby, wake up," I said as I pulled the covers off her naked body.

I stared down at her naked body and smiled. Just looking at her was about to get my dick hard.

"I said wake up," I told her as I smacked her ass.

Shiya rolled over and smiled.

"You know I like that shit, right?"

"I know you do." I smiled back.

She arched her back, put her phat ass in the air, and began slowly twerking for me so that I could see her ass cheeks jiggle and clap.

"Don't start something you can't finish," I said, stroking my dick through my pants

"Oh, I definitely intend to finish anything I start, baby."

Shiya rolled over onto her back, lifted her legs, and then spread them for me. I watched her rub on her titties and then make her way down to her soft, pink pussy. I pulled my shirt off over my head and unleashed my hard ass dick that was dying to get out of my pants. She crawled over to the edge of the bed and slid my dick into her warm mouth. Shiya was a pro at sucking dick. I loved the gurgling and gagging sounds she made and the fact that she would never once throw up or quit. She held the base of my dick with her right hand and let me fuck the back of her throat.

"Mmm... shit," I said, palming the back of her head.

"You like that shit, baby?" she asked, coming up for air.

"Hell yeah. I love that shit. Come put that pussy on my face, baby."

I laid down, and she climbed on top of me, straddling my face. I ate her pussy and then slid from underneath her to turn her over on her back. I climbed on top of her and kissed her roughly. Our tongues swirled around in each other's mouths before I made my way down to suck on her hard nipples. She used to be an A cup but begged me to get her breasts done a few years ago to turn her into a D cup. I didn't mind. They looked good and they felt soft, so that was all I cared about.

Shiya crawled on all fours and propped her ass up in the air for me. She knew what time it was. I got down on my knees and took her ass in both hands then licked her pussy from behind once more before entering her pussy from behind. I was thoroughly enjoying the view of her twerking on my dick. I grabbed her small waist, pulled her onto my hard dick, and started plowing into her.

"Just like that, baby," I said as she bounced her ass back against my dick.

I loved it when she fucked me back. It was sexy. I grabbed her waist tightly and drilled into her pussy while fingering her tight asshole. She gasped and then moaned.

"Mmm... Shit, baby."

"Goddamn, this shit is so fucking wet, Shiya." I groaned.

"Mmm. Only for you, baby," she assured me.

We switched positions, and I climbed on top of her. She propped herself up on one elbow and I held onto her left leg that was resting on my shoulder. I palmed the back of her neck with my free hand and continued to fuck her.

"Mmm... Don't stop, Law!"

"You about to cum, baby?"

"Yesss!"

The harder I fucked her, the louder she got. I knew everybody in the house could hear her screams of pleasure, but I didn't give a fuck. I watched as she threw her expensive Brazilian weave to the side and looked at me as she took my dick. I wrapped my hands around her neck as I thrust into her.

"Mmm... shit. You love me, baby?" she asked.

"Yeah, I love you," I told her.

"Mmm... I love you too and this dick, baby. I love this dick!"

"You gon' cum all over this dick, baby?" I asked, feeling myself about to climax.

I smacked her ass, and she moaned and nodded. She reached back and spread her left ass cheek so that I could go deeper. You see, most niggas thought that good dick was the only thing that made a woman cum. In reality, it was loyalty, too. Shiya knew my dick was hers, and that made her a freak for me and only me.

"Mmm... fuck! Shit! Law beat this pussy up, baby!" She screamed.

"I want you to cum all over this dick, baby. It's your dick, right?"

"Mmm, yes. It's my dick. I'm gonna cum all over my dick!" She squealed.

Two strokes later, Shiya's body began shaking non-stop as she rode the wave of her orgasm. I followed right along behind her. I came all over her ass, and she rubbed it all over her wet pussy. I fucking loved her freaky ass. The two of us collapsed on the bed, breathing heavily.

"You were being extra loud this morning, baby," I told her.

"I know. Just in case there were a few listening ears, I had to let them know who your dick belonged to."

I shook my head. Nashiya had a terrible jealous streak, especially when it came to Raquel.

"Look, I need you to roll with me in a couple hours to go see Al."

"Aww, baby. I can't."

"What do you mean you can't? Since when do you ever say no to me?" I asked.

"Since I told you I was going out of town this weekend to visit my sister in Cali. And to check on the connect out there and see what he's talkin' about."

"I don't need you sticking your nose all in my business like that, Shiya. You know I hate that shit."

"I know. I'm not setting up a meeting with the nigga; I'm just putting my ears to the streets. Al is cool and all, but his ass is old, and you already know with all this beef between you and them pussy ass Price boys, there's going to come a time where he drops you. Then what?"

"He wouldn't do that. He's been fucking with my family for too long to do that."

"Yeah, and he's probably been fucking with the Price family for the same amount of time. His loyalty ain't to either one of y'all. You need a fallback plan."

"Fine," I said, giving up.

I didn't want to argue, and I didn't want to hear anything else she had to say. It was pointless if she wasn't going to be standing by my side when I needed her to.

"You'll be fine," she said as she kissed my sweaty neck.

"Yeah, sure. You're right. I got it." I nodded.

"I'm about to get in the shower and get ready to head to the airport, baby."

"Okay. Have a safe flight."

"I love you, Law."

"I love you too, Shiya."

As soon as Shiya pulled off, I went back in the house and knocked on Raquel's bedroom door.

"Who is it?"

"It's Law. Open the door."

I waited a few seconds for her to open the door.

"You're coming with me today," I told her.

"Where are we going?"

"You ask a lot of questions."

"How else am I supposed to get answers if I don't ask questions?"

"We're meeting with a business partner of mine this afternoon on his yacht. Shiya is on her way out of town and can't come, and I need to look like I'm relaxing with my lady and not doing business, so you're taking her place today. Be ready in an hour."

* * *

Raquel

Law and I stepped outside and got into a blacked-out Mercedes. It was so damn sexy. The tint was dark as night with black rims to match. It was like riding around the streets of Miami in the Batmobile. I kept my attention focused on everything that we were passing as Law sped down the interstate doing no less than 100 miles per hour. He kept the music bumping loud until he turned it down at a red light and looked over at me.

"You aight?" he asked.

"Yeah. I'm fine," I nodded.

"Good."

"Can I say something?"

"Depends on what it is."

"Why bring me here today? Like, why not just reschedule with this business partner of yours for another day when your girl was available? I'm sure you know Nashiya don't like me, right?"

"What do you mean?"

"Don't act like you haven't seen the hate in her face when she looks at me or when you or someone else mentions my name. I make her sick, and I have no reason why."

"I don't know nothing about that female shit. Why don't you just ask her? That's what I do when I feel like a nigga got a problem with me."

"Because I really don't care that much." I shrugged. "Besides, she made it perfectly clear y'all are doing just fine with all that goddamn hollering she was doing this morning like you were drilling a fucking hole in her back."

"Damn, you heard that shit? I told her ass she was being loud as hell."

"I'm pretty sure people in Texas heard how loud she was," I said, folding my arms.

"I don't know. She probably thinks you want me or something." He shrugged.

"Want you? Why would I want you?" I asked, scrunching up my forehead, utterly confused.

"Why wouldn't you want me?" he asked nonchalantly.

"Okay, I get it. Here's the part where you become Mr. Cocky. Well, you can go right on somewhere with all that shit."

I threw up my hand and turned my attention back out the window to watch all the sites zooming by.

"I'm just saying. From her perspective, the higher you level up in this game, the different breeds of women you attract. Her nigga has it all and females see that and they want to take her place."

"I mean, I guess I get it, but she should know she has nothing to worry about. You're not anywhere near my type."

"Oh, I'm not? What exactly is your type then, Raquel?" he said, glancing over at me.

"Hmm... let's see... tall, smart, funny, level-headed, gorgeous body, face, and skin. That type of stuff."

"You do know you just described me, right?" He smirked.

"And not the leader of a goddamn crime family. How about that?" I added.

Law chuckled.

"Shut up, yo."

Law continued to drive while I looked out the window in silence. I turned to look at him when he brought the car to a complete stop.

"Where exactly are we?"

"Biscayne Bay," he answered.

I nodded.

"And what exactly am I supposed to do?"

"You don't do anything. You sit, you smile, and most importantly, you don't listen. Tune us out. Do whatever you gotta do. Just don't fuck this shit up for me."

"I won't."

Law got out of the car and walked over to open my door.

"You're such a gentleman," I said sarcastically while quickly rolling my eyes.

Law cut his eyes at me and then grabbed me by the hand.

"C'mon. Let's go."

I tugged on the hem of my short dress with my free hand, hoping to pull it down a bit. A part of me felt like a prostitute, but I knew I was just a prop. I put some sunglasses over my eyes and looked around while letting the vitamin D soak into my skin. It was a bright and sunny day with not a cloud in sight. The palm trees were swaying gently in the warm breeze. There were dozens of people walking around, getting on yachts and just enjoying themselves in the nice weather.

"Watch your step," Law said, bringing me back to reality.

He stepped onto the bridge that took us from mainland over onto the large, white yacht with the word *Venus* written on the side in script and grabbed my hand to help me. When we were both safely onboard, Law let go of my hand to dap up a large Hispanic man in a black suit.

"What's up? Is Al ready for me?"

"Is this your lady?" the man asked.

"Yeah, she's with me," he said, grabbing my hand once again.

"Al is at the dining room table downstairs having brunch. You can go ahead down there," he told us.

Law nodded and guided us into the large, three-level yacht. It was so beautiful. My eyes were starting to glaze over.

"Law, I'm so happy you could make it," an older Hispanic man with salt and pepper hair said as he stood to shake his hand.

"What's up, Al?"

"And who is this lovely señorita you have accompanying you today?" he asked with a heavy Spanish accent.

"This is Raquel, a friend of the family."

Alistair looked at me and flashed a wide smile. His teeth were nice and white. They were almost too perfect to be naturally his. Then again, by the looks of his yacht, he had money to spend on anything he wanted. A colorful Hawaiian-print shirt covered his mid-size frame, and he wore a pair of khaki shorts and boat shoes.

"Hi," I said, extending my hand.

"Hello, beautiful. It is very nice to meet you," he said as he kissed my hand.

"It's nice to meet you, too."

"Please, both of you take a seat. Would you like something to drink? A mimosa perhaps?" Al asked.

I nodded.

"Yes, a mimosa would be nice. Thank you."

They say first impressions are lasting, and Alistair had sure made one on me. He was so polite. I didn't know how anyone involved in the drug game could be so nice and well mannered, but I was sure he had a dark side to him, just like Law did. I sat perfectly still with my leg gently crossed over the other and waited for my mimosa. I noticed there was a chessboard off to the side of the onyx black table. It had glass pieces and looked like the game wasn't done.

"You play chess?" I asked.

"I sure do. It's the best game to strengthen your mind. I play against myself at least once a day. It's always good to know what your opponent is thinking so that you can figure out how to make your next move your best move."

"I like that."

"Maybe we can play someday. I'm always up for some friendly competition."

"Maybe so." I smiled.

Al turned to Law and smiled.

"She's a keeper. I like her."

"Thank you," he nodded.

"Would the two of you like a quick tour before we get down to business?"

I looked at Law who nodded and then looked back at Al.

"Yes, of course."

"Great. So for starters, this is the dining area. There is a glass bar over there. I love mirrors, so I really wanted as much glass as possible. It's beautiful to look at but a real son of a bitch to keep clean. Lucky for me, I have people who take care of that for me."

Al continued to walk us through his yacht. There were seven suites, all accessible with a unique fingerprint pad for his guests. Each bathroom had a Jacuzzi tub in it. There were three swimming pools on board, one being a massage pool near the stern of the boat with his and her massage chairs. I noticed the drink holders in between the seats and that the bottom of the pool was all glass. He showed us the personal movie theater, state-of-the-art gym, and the helipad on the bow of the boat. His yacht came equipped with twenty-three crewmembers, a chef, and personal house cleaner. He was truly living the good life.

"Your yacht is beautiful," I told him.

"Thank you. I love the water, so I figured why not have a custom-built, twenty-one million dollar home on it?"

"Wise man." I smiled.

"I'd like to think so too." He smiled back.

The three of us sat in silence for a bit, listening to the waves crash into the side of the luxurious boat.

"Are you ready to get down to business, Law?" Alistair asked, breaking the silence.

"Yeah." He nodded.

"Raquel, please enjoy the pool and all the other amenities my water home has to offer. Go outside and soak up some sun while Law and I talk man to man. It won't take long," he assured me.

"Thank you again for your hospitality." I smiled.

* * *

Alistair and I stepped into his private office on the lower level of the yacht, leaving Raquel out on the boat in one of the lounge chairs by the swimming pool.

"First, let me say that I was very sorry to hear about your brother's death."

"Thank you." I nodded.

"I wanted to make it to the funeral, but I was away on business. Did you receive my gift?"

"Yeah. We uh... We got the flowers and the food. Thank you."

"You know, in my country, we celebrate death. You Americans do things so differently here. We bring the deceased to the family home, light candles, and visitors will come and stay to pay their respects, to mourn, to eat, everything. Then we pray."

I nodded. I guess he wasn't accustomed to the way black funerals went. We still ate and prayed. We just didn't do it all inside the house. We made sure my brother went out in style with a fourteen karat gold casket.

"Did you handle our little problem?" Alistair asked me as he took a seat behind his desk.

"It's been taken care of," I assured him.

"And that girl you brought with you, who is she really?"

"I already told you. She's just a family friend."

"I meant what I said, Law. I like her. She's good for business. I know you love your fiancée, but we both know that girl is... how do you say... rough around the edges."

"Look, with all due respect, I didn't come here to talk about my love life. I came here to talk about what's going on in these streets. Now, with the shit that popped off a few weeks ago, it was on some eye for an eye shit, nothin' else. Those fuckin' Price boys took it there, so we brought the shit right back to their doorstep. Shit should be quiet for a while now."

"You really think things are going to be quiet? There's two of you left and there's two of them left. None of you are going to stop until the others are dead. That shit is bad for my business!" he said through clenched teeth.

"How so?" I asked with a hard look on my face.

"I supply you, Law. I've been supplying your family since your father was running things. The rivalry you've got is too hot right now. I'm not getting mixed up in the middle of this shit! How long before someone comes fishing around about the murder and then links your drugs to me? I've been in this game a very long time, and I refuse to go down over two sets of boys having a pissing match."

"What do you suggest?" I asked, adjusting myself in the chair across from him.

"I'll arrange a sit down between the two of you and the two of them. Come to an agreement. No more bloodshed for the sake of everybody involved, okay?"

"A fucking sit down? Hell no! Nobody is going to agree to that shit."

"At the end of the day all you mothafuckas should be worried about is getting money and staying the fuck out of jail and a casket. You want my drugs, you take my advice. Make it fucking happen. I'll be sending a shipment to the warehouse in two days."

I exhaled and clenched my jaw. I felt like my hands were tied. For as far back as I could remember it had always been beef between the Calloway and the Price families. Whether it was over drug territory, money, or women, it didn't matter. All I knew was Miami wasn't big enough for both of us to come together on no kumbaya shit.

"Set it up. Blaze and I will be there."

"I'm going to tell you like I'll tell them, leave the fucking guns and the bullshit at the door, or I'll have my guys wipe out the Callaways and the Prices, feel me?"

Alistair knew I didn't take too kindly to threats, but I decided to let it go. Truth was I didn't have time to go hunting for another plug, but I was going to check in with Shiya about seeing what was going on over on the west coast where her sister lived. If shit at this sit down didn't go well, she was right. I was going to need a plan B.

"Got it." I nodded.

"Good. Now, I've got some business on land to take care of. You and your *family friend* can have my boat for the rest of the day if you wish to enjoy yourselves in whatever ways you want."

"Thanks. I'll let her know."

The two of us stood to our feet at the same time and shook hands. I walked outside on the deck to find Raquel doing exactly what Alistair had suggested, soaking up sun. She looked peaceful. Her light-brown skin already had a nice bronze glow to it.

"All done?" she asked as she lifted her sunglasses to look at me.

"Yeah. All done."

"Damn, that was pretty quick."

"We told you it would be."

"Yeah, but I thought that was just man talk and you were really going to be back there for an hour or more. I was just getting comfortable."

"Well, he did say we could have the boat for the rest of the day if we wanted."

"Really?" she squealed.

I chuckled and nodded.

"Yeah, really."

"Well, I'm down if you are. It's not like I get too many opportunities to get out of the house these days."

I could hear the hint of sarcasm in her voice, but decided to let it go. I sat down on one of the chairs across from her and rested my head in my hands. There was no way Blaze or those motherfucking Prices were going to go for a peaceful sit down. I just knew it. I didn't trust those niggas at all, and I never would. Whenever we were around each other bodies were going to fall. I knew I had to figure out a game plan and fast.

"Got a lot on your mind?" she asked, interrupting my train of thought.

"Always."

"Like what?"

"I don't want to talk about it, Raquel."

"Okay. Well, then how about you tell me something that nobody knows about you."

"Why?" I shrugged.

"Because I want to know."

"You go first."

"I don't think you'd believe me if I told you," she said as she looked away.

"Try me."

"Well, for starters, I'm a virgin."

"Wait. A what? Like you've never had sex before?"

"That's typically how people define a virgin. Yes." She nodded.

"Why not?"

I knew my question was personal, but I didn't give a fuck. I was shocked. I didn't think I'd ever met a virgin in my life, and if I had, she definitely wasn't in her twenties. I had to know her reasoning behind it.

"Well, I was saving myself for marriage. I was actually engaged for a year and a half, and I planned to get married to my ex, Derrick, in six months."

"What happened?"

"A week before I came down here on vacation, I caught him fucking my roommate, who was also going to be my maid of honor, in my apartment."

"Shit. That's savage as fuck."

"I know, right? He was supposed to have been a virgin too, but as you can see, he lied about that."

"Well, If he didn't fight for you, he never wanted you in the first place in my opinion..."

"You're right. I guess losing him was my biggest win in some twisted ass way."

"Pretty much." I nodded.

"All I ever wanted was for someone to feel for me what I felt for them, somebody who was going to put in the same amount of effort, you know? That 'I love you to the moon and back,' type of love, but that's just now how life goes I guess." She shrugged and huffed.

"So, why hold onto it? Why not just lose it and get it over with?"

"Believe me. I've thought about it plenty of times, but I just haven't found anyone who makes me want to give it to them."

"And what exactly are you looking for?"

"I don't know." She shrugged. "But when I find him, I'll know."

"So, wait. Not to be all in your business or anything, but if you've never had sex before, what have you done?"

"Are you asking me if I masturbate, Law?" She smirked.

"Uh, yeah. I guess I am."

"Yes, I masturbate. I just don't stick anything inside me. I'm not a child. I know how to make myself cum repeatedly. I've gotten head. I've just never been penetrated before with anything more than a finger or two."

"Damn, that's crazy. I've really been sitting here this entire time trying to think if I've ever met a virgin in my life."

"First time for everything, huh?" She chuckled.

"Yeah, I guess so," I said, laughing with her.

"You still never answered my question, though."

"And what question was that?"

"What is something that nobody knows about you?" she asked.

I sat and contemplated for a few seconds. There was a bunch of shit people didn't know about me. I liked keeping my life as mysterious as possible. The less people knew, the less they could tell.

"Um, let's see. My mind is like a tornado sometimes...just a whirlwind of thoughts and emotions."

"Happens to the best of us," she assured me.

* * *

Raquel

Law and I continued to talk for hours. We laughed and joked together, too. As serious as he was, I could tell that deep down, underneath that hard ass exterior, he really was a good person.

"So where are you from?" he asked me.

"Guess."

"Anywhere but here," he shrugged.

"Nice, smart ass. I'm originally from Hawaii believe it or not. I was born over there and lived there until I was about five then my dad got stationed in South Carolina. I've been there ever since."

"You go to college or anything like that?"

"Yeah. I actually just graduated from Alabama State University a few weeks before I came down here."

"Wow. That's dope. What'd you go for?"

"I double majored in mass communications and business management. I want to open up my own law firm one day. Next step after graduation was to apply for law school, but I was going to wait until after I got married, but you see how that ended up for me."

"Yeah." He nodded.

"What about you? Where'd you go to school?"

"Miami Senior High School. I ain't no college boy like what you're used to, but I did think about maybe going to community college one day."

"What happened with that?"

"I just got caught up in the money and shit. If you haven't noticed, school doesn't really fit into the life I'm living."

"You can always go back whenever you want. There's no age or time limit on getting your education if it's something you're real serious about."

Law laughed.

"How would that look? A nigga like me with a book bag and doing homework by day, then managing the family business at night."

"Anything is possible, Law."

"So, uh, you got any siblings?" he asked, changing the subject.

"No. Just me. My parents got it right the first time. No offense."

"None taken."

"I feel like I'm rambling or something."

"Nah, it's cool. I'm no social butterfly, but I like hearing you talk," he assured me.

"You do, huh?"

"Yeah, I do."

I flashed him a quick smile and then looked him over. His arms and hands were covered in tattoos.

"You like my tattoos?" he asked.

"Sorry for staring... But yeah, what's that on your hand? Is it a compass?"

"Yup."

"What does that mean?"

"Basically, the purpose of a compass is to lead you in the right direction, right? So, I got it to symbolize that no matter what I faced, I would always lead myself in the right direction to find my way back home to my family."

"Wow, that's actually really deep."

"What about you? Do you have any tattoos?"

"One."

"Where is it?"

"My thigh. It's a bunch of roses. I love roses."

"True." He nodded.

"You know one thing I've noticed about you?"

"What?"

"I notice you try to be alone a lot."

"Sometimes being alone is best," he said.

"Why?"

"It's always better than being around fake mothafuckas or niggas with they hands held out all the time."

"Mmm... shit," I said, holding my stomach.

"You okay?"

"I think the boat is starting to make me a little sea sick or something."

"Aw shit. If you gon' throw up ,you need to do it now and not in my car."

"I'm not going to throw up. I don't think."

"Let's go then so you can get back to the house."

"Good idea." I nodded.

Law and I walked off the boat and back onto mainland. We got back in the car, and he sped off.

CHAPTER NINE

Raquel

I woke up to the sound of Nashiya's annoying ass voice projecting throughout the house like she was talking into a loudspeaker. She and Law were arguing again. They'd been doing it a lot since I showed up. To me, Nashiya was nothing but a jealous ass bitch. I rolled over onto my back and listened to their argument with my eyes closed, trying to go back to sleep.

"You got me all the way fucked up if you think I don't know what the fuck is going on here, Law. I can see right through all this petty bullshit. Are you fucking this bitch? Is that what's going on?"

"Shiya, I swear to God you better calm down before you make me get out of character," he told her as his baritone voice ripped through the air.

"Jump out of character then, nigga! If you feelin' froggy, then leap! Like I said, you got me fucked up!"

"What the fuck do you even mean by that shit, girl?"

"Nigga, you owe me!"

"Owe you? What the fuck do I owe you? I pay all your

fucking bills, and I put that big ass ring on your fucking finger! You better get the fuck out of my face with that bullshit, Shiya. I'm not playing!"

"Shut the fuck up, Law. I say whatever the fuck I want!"

"Nah, you wanted a trap nigga, right? That's what you said when you first started fuckin' with me, so I turned you into my trap bitch, and now what? Huh? What the fuck else do you want from me, Shiya?"

"Trap bitch! That's how you're carrying it now, Law? Huh? I want you to stop fucking lying to me, and tell me you fuckin' the bitch. Just because I wasn't available, you gon' take that bitch to meet your fucking plug? That's what we do now, Law?"

"I'm not fucking her, Shiya! Damn!"

"Then if you not fucking her, I can go ask her."

"Ask her what? I just fucking told you that I'm not fuckin' her. What more do you want?"

"I want the fuckin' truth, and I'm not gon' stop until I get it!"

"So, what you really tellin' me is you don't fuckin' trust me."

"It's not you I don't trust. It's that bitch. What the fuck, Law? Are you stupid? The bitch ain't blind, and I know her yellow ass ain't lickin' no pussy, so I know she got her nose all wide open for your ass!"

* * *

It seemed like Law needed to be reminded that I was born at night but not last night. He and that bitch Raquel had me all the way fucked up. She had his nose wide open, and I could see it from a mile away. I didn't know why he couldn't. I walked up to Raquel's door and banged on it, not caring if I woke up the whole damn house.

"Open the motherfucking door, bitch!"

I could've slapped the shit out of her as soon as I saw the smirk written across her face.

"Good morning. What's up?" she asked.

"Wipe that look off your face before I wipe it off for you, bitch!"

"What is going on?" she asked, rubbing her eyes.

"Don't play dumb, bitch. You may have got everybody else around this mothafucka fooled, but not me. Now somebody is going to tell me the truth around this bitch before I really go the fuck off!"

"What do you want to know?"

"What do I want to know? You know exactly what the fuck I want to know! Don't play dumb with me, bitch! Are you fucking my man?"

"No. I'm not," she said, shaking her head.

"See? I told you," Law interjected.

I looked back at Law and then at Raquel. I didn't believe either one of their lying asses.

"So neither one of you want to tell me the truth, huh?"

"Nashiya, I just told you I'm not checking for your man, okay?" she said. "Honest to God, we haven't had sex. We haven't kissed. We haven't done anything. I put that on my life."

I stepped up to her and put my pointer finger to the side of her head.

"And if I ever find out different, that's exactly what you'll pay with—your fucking life, bitch."

I stormed off down the hall before I wrapped my hands

around her pretty little throat. I didn't stop until I was seated behind the driver's seat of my Barbie-pink Mercedes. I pressed the button to start the engine and pulled off with my tires spinning.

"Siri, call Janique."

I listened to the phone ring three times before Janique's voice came through the car speakers.

"Hello?"

"Nique, what are you doing?"

"About to take Trey to the babysitter, a.k.a. his grandmother's house. I need a break, bitch."

I chuckled a little bit and then went right back to being mad as hell.

"I need to run something by you."

"What's up, girl?" she asked.

"You remember back when you and Petey were together and you caught him cheating... Did he let on to any hints or anything before you found out?"

"Girl, all Petey's ass did was cheat. He was a full-time cheater, the CEO of cheating nigga enterprises! So, what are you talking about?" she said, smacking her lips together.

I exhaled deeply and shook my head.

"Hold up, is this about that little light-skinned bitch that's been at your house?" she asked me.

"That's exactly who it's about."

"You caught Law fucking her?"

"No, I didn't."

"Then what's up? You worried about her getting too close to Law or something?"

"I confronted the both of them just a few minutes ago and asked them flat out if they were fucking, and they both denied it, but I just don't know."

"Hold up, so you pulled out the crazy Shiya on both of their asses?"

"Hell yeah, I did, and I'd do it again, too. I told that bitch from day one not to fuck with my man. I can just feel it in me. I know something is going on I just can't put my finger on it!"

"He told you to your face that he's not fucking her though, right?"

"Yeah, but you know just as well as I do niggas lie for fun!"

"Nah, not Petey's ass. Shit, anytime I asked him if he was cheating, he came right out and told my ass hell yeah he was. His ho ass even had the nerve to ask me if I wanted to join! And my ass was pregnant with Trey at the time!"

"That's disgusting," I said, screwing up my face and shaking my head.

"But that's a thought though."

"What?"

"A threesome."

"Are you fucking kidding me, bitch? I'm not doing that shit."

"I'm not necessarily telling you to do it. I'm just saying. You're way too close to getting married to let some bitch that dropped out of the sky steal your man. If you think he wants her, maybe invite her into y'all bedroom. That way he gets it out of his system and you're not the one being left in the dark."

"Law's not that type of nigga. He's always been satisfied with me and only me."

"If that's the case, then why are your suspicions on a thousand right now?" she asked.

I sighed. She was right. Law had never given me a reason not to trust him in the five years we'd been together. It really was Raquel I didn't trust, but at the end of the day, she didn't have anything to do with our relationship. I was the one with the ring. I was the one who Law was fucking raw damn near every night. And I was going to be the one to have his last name and bear his children, not her.

"I don't know... I really don't."

"So, calm your black ass down. If you checked the bitch and his ass, all should be good going forward. If she's as timid as you said she is, she'll be too scared to get her pussy wet around him," Janique joked.

"I'm gonna keep checking this bitch every chance I get, too. Believe that."

"Hey. Ain't nothin' wrong with protecting what's yours. That's your man, and you've got the right to do that."

"Thanks, girl. I really needed that."

"Anytime, boo. You my girl. You know I got you."

I pressed the button on my touch screen inside the car to disconnect the call. Janique had been my girl since high school. She was one of the few I confided in when it came to Law and our relationship. She was a real bitch, and I appreciated her outlook on things. She gave it to me raw and uncut just how I needed it. Shit, it didn't matter how pretty Raquel was. I wasn't above fucking her face up. I warned her twice about fucking with what was mine, and I didn't want to have to do it for a third time, but I would if I had to. Janique was right, I was too close to my wedding date, and I was not about to allow that bitch to fuck up what I had.

* * *

Raquel

I couldn't believe the way Nashiya's ass came at me. I knew she thought I was just going to roll over and take her shit every time she threw it my way, but I wasn't. I made a promise to myself that the next time she came at me on some bullshit would be her last. I spent the rest of the day locked in my room with a bad ass attitude. I hadn't even noticed it had gotten dark until I got up to use the bathroom. When I was on my way back to the bed, there was a knock at the door.

I walked over and swung it open, ready to give anybody standing on the other side a piece of my mind.

"Law... What are you doing here?" I asked, holding onto the doorknob.

"I just wanted to apologize for Shiya's behavior earlier today. The shit was out of line and uncalled for."

"Thanks." I nodded.

"You busy?"

"What could I really be doing besides planning my next escape?" I asked, sarcastically.

"Can I come in? You know... to talk?"

"Where is your fiancée?"

"She's not here. Don't worry about her. I got her. She won't come at you sideways anymore. I promise."

"Mmhm. Yeah... sure." I nodded.

"So..."

"Yeah. Come in."

Law walked past me and headed right out onto the balcony. I followed behind him and closed the door behind us.

"So, what's up? What's wrong? What did you want to talk about?" I asked with my arms folded across my chest.

"I don't know," he shrugged.

"There's clearly something going on in that head of yours."

Law sighed.

"You ever hit a point where you just don't give a fuck about any of the things you used to? That's where my head is stuck at right now."

"Explain."

"For one, Shiya is getting on my nerves. I ain't got time for this jealous ass shit. I got enough shit on my plate than to come here and have to listen to her bitch and complain about some shit I'm not even doing."

"What exactly is she complaining about?" I asked.

"I think the better question is what doesn't she complain about. I just wanna smoke a little bit, clear my mind, and sip on somethin' to mellow me the fuck out, and then maybe I can deal with her ass."

"Is it really that bad?"

"She expects too much and gives too little. All I ever wanted was a bitch... I mean a female... who could see past the money and the drugs and guns and all that shit, and I just think that the closer we get to this wedding, the cloudier her judgment is getting by the fuckin' day."

"So why are you marrying her?"

Law sighed and looked at me then puffed his blunt.

"You ever smoke before?" he asked, changing the subject.

"No. I haven't," I said, shaking my head.

"Here, hit it just once."

"I don't know..."

"C'mon. You're safe with me. You should know that by now."

"I mean, I don't know how to smoke. What do I do?"

"Put the tip of it in your mouth and inhale deep to let the smoke fill your lungs. Once you've got some in there, hold your breath for a few seconds then slowly push the air out of your nose or mouth. Whatever works for you."

"Like this?" I asked, puffing the blunt and holding my breath.

I immediately coughed as the smoke danced around inside my lungs, rattling my entire body and setting my chest on fire.

"What the fuck, Law!"

Law laughed at me and took his blunt back before I dropped it.

"You're hilarious. You know that?"

"I'm glad you've gotten a laugh at my expense!" I said, holding my chest.

"I'm not laughing at you. I'm laughing with you."

"I'm not laughing, though!"

"You're right." He nodded. "I apologize."

"But back to what we were talking about..."

"And what was that again?"

"You and Nashiya and why she's getting on your nerves."

"I don't know what her damn problem is sometimes."

"You may not know her problem, but I know yours."

"Me? I don't have no problem."

"Yes, you do."

"What is it then?"

"I know that Nashiya is a... different breed of woman, but I think we as women all want the same thing at the end of the day."

"Which is?" he asked, cutting me off.

"Which is someone who can give us more than just roses or luxurious things. Roses die. You blow money like it's going out of style around here. What would you do if you woke up tomorrow and it was all gone? Would you still be able to provide for her? What would you give her instead of money, Law? I truly don't think you know."

It was the first time I found myself taking Nashiya's side, which was something I never thought I'd do in a million years, especially after the way she'd just came at me.

"You're right. I don't know, but I don't know because she's never asked for anything else."

"Why do you think that is?"

"Nashiya is... different. She knew she hooked a boss the moment she met me. She's told me that hundreds of times. To you, she may look like a gold digger, but what you don't see is that she's been down from the first day I met her."

"So you reward her loyalty with an engagement ring?"

"And a promise that as long as she continues to be loyal to me,

I'll do the same for her... but I don't know, man. It be little shit sometimes that make me raise an eyebrow."

"Little things like what?" I asked.

"Like for one, she keeps blowing up my phone and sending me pictures and shit."

"Pictures of what?"

"Wedding stuff. That's all she cares about! I keep telling her anything she pick is fine with me. I've got bigger shit to worry about besides that."

"Do you even want to get married, Law? Like really?"

"Why you ask me that?"

"Do you not hear yourself and the way you're talking? You're about to make a commitment in front of God and your family to love this woman and be with her for the rest of your life and you're brushing everything off like it's just another day."

"Because that's exactly what it is," he shrugged. "It's like that to all men. Everybody knows a wedding is just for the woman anyway."

"Sounds like you're rushing into it if you ask me."

"Maybe we are." He shrugged.

"Then why do it? You two have the rest of your lives to get married. You can't rush something that you want to last forever. You do want your marriage to last forever, right?" I asked.

When Law didn't respond to me, I asked a follow up question.

"You don't even love her, do you?"

"I care about her. I really do."

"Caring about someone and loving someone are two different things, Law. Love is simple to me. If I feel like it's not flowing naturally, then it probably isn't meant to be, and I think you're wise enough to know that."

"And I think you're wise enough to mind your fucking business," he said, getting up and heading for the door.

"Law, wait. I didn't mean to upset you. I'm just trying to help you!"

"Help me? Ain't nobody ever helped me. How the fuck are you helping me, Raquel?"

"I'm trying to stop you from making the biggest mistake of your life, and you know it!"

"I think my biggest mistake thus far was sparing your ass. Remember your place in all this, and play your role," he said, leaving me standing outside on the balcony dumbfounded.

CHAPTER TEN

Lan

After the door closed behind me, I immediately regretted talking to Raquel the way I did. I was just too stressed about the fucking sit down and all the shit I had going on with Nashiya to want to hear anything she had to say, even if it was the truth. A part of me wished that I could've told her that I valued her opinion more than some other people who had been around me damn near all my life. I knew it couldn't be like that, though. Raquel had her place in my life, and she wasn't the number one woman. Nashiya was the woman I was going to bless with my last name and my children. Too much had happened between us for me to change my mind and break her heart all because of one woman, even if I did have feelings for her.

I put all the other thoughts aside and focused back on what had really been at the forefront of my mind; the sit down with Alistair, Blaze, the Price brothers, and myself.

"Hey, B, you got a second?" I asked, knocking on his already half way open door.

"Sup?"

"I need to holla at you about somethin' real quick."

Blaze nodded and I closed the door behind me. I knew Blaze hated anybody with the last name Price just as much as I did if not more, so I knew he wasn't going to take the news of Alistair's sit down well.

"So, what's up?" he asked.

"I met with Al a couple days ago. He said the shipment will be coming into the warehouse tonight."

"Okay, cool."

"He also asked about our situation with the Price brothers."

"What about them mothafuckas?" he asked with a Grimm look across his face.

"He wants us to have a sit down with them and call a truce on all the killing. He doesn't want the heat to blow back on him."

"I don't give a fuck about what he wants. I'm not sittin' down with those niggas!"

"I know, and I told him that, but until we find another plug, he's all we got. We gotta play by his rules right now if we wanna keep makin' money."

"Man, fuck this shit, yo!" he said, turning his back to me.

"Look, I get exactly where you're coming from. I do, but at the end of the day, we gotta put our feelings to the side and handle business on this get money shit, aight? This is king shit we on, nigga. Those pussy ass Price boys wouldn't know nothin' 'bout that. All we gotta do is sit and listen and don't agree to shit."

Blaze cut his eyes at me and then shook his head.

"When?"

"Alistair called me earlier. We're meeting tonight in an hour."

"A fucking hour and you're just now telling me about this?"

"I know. Just trust me on this shit, aight? I got you," I assured him.

"You got me, and I got my gun."

"Leave that shit in the car, Blaze. He already made it clear he don't want us or them brining any heat to the sit down."

"And let them niggas murder us like they did Wolfe? C'mon now, Law. I know you've got to be smarter than that."

"You're not hearing me! I told you that this shit is bigger than any beef we got goin' on right now, aight? It's business. That's it."

Blaze brushed me off as he put his hoodie on and placed his gun in the back of his jeans.

"For precaution. That's it." He shrugged, mocking me.

I shook my head and looked him up and down. My baby brother was really growing up. He was still wild, but I could tell he was comin' into his own. I prayed nothing happened to me anytime soon for his sake and the sake of the family business. I knew he couldn't handle it yet. Blaze was a different type of nigga. He didn't have much of a heart, but every move he made was based off his emotions, and that was bad for business. I threw my arm around his shoulder, and the two of us went downstairs and got in the car. As soon as I pressed the button to start it, I got a text message from Al.

Al: 3910 Collins Ave.

Law: Bet.

I put the car in drive and sped off. When we arrived, we parked on the side of the street and waited. A few minutes passed before I saw a black SUV pull up and park on the street directly across from us. As soon as the vehicle lights shut off, I saw Darius and Dallas Price hop out of the vehicle and walk into the club where the five of us were supposed to meet.

"Let's go. It's show time," I told Blaze.

The two of us hopped out of the car and made our way into the night club. We didn't stop until we got to the back of the club in a private VIP section. Dallas and Darius were sitting across from us, while Alistair stood there with a glass filled with liquor in his hand.

"Ah. At last, the Calloway men are here." Alistair smiled as he took a sip from his glass. "Please, have a seat."

Blaze and I looked at each other and then sat across from Darius and Dallas. Alistair took his seat at the head of the table and looked at the four of us.

"Thank you for putting your pride to the side and agreeing to this sit down."

The four of us sat in silence and stared each other down.

"Fuck are we really here for, Al?" Dallas asked as he pushed his dreads out of his face.

"Your brother Damien is dead and so is their brother, Wolfe. The killing needs to stop now. No more!"

"Man, fuck them niggas," Darius said as he stood up and grabbed his dick.

"Fuck us? Nigga, fuck you!" Blaze said as he stood to his feet and reached around for his gun.

I quickly stood beside him and put my hand on his arm to stop him from exposing his gun. I cursed myself on the inside for even agreeing to the sit down in the first place because I knew Blaze's temper wouldn't allow him to handle it the way I needed him to. There was too much wildness still lingering inside his body.

"Yo, chill," I whispered to him.

"Nah. Fuck that. I'm a certified thug out here, nigga. I'll shoot the smile off your mothafuckin' face, you hear me? It's not just talk when you can back it up, and niggas know that about me, pussy ass nigga!" Blaze yelled.

"Here the fuckin' baby golden boy go, huffin' and puffin' and talkin' big shit," Darius said as he brushed him off.

"Are the two of you done with your pissing match yet? If so, we can get back down to business," Al interjected.

"We're ready," I said, pulling Blaze back down into his seat.

"Look, fellas, I like you both. I really do, but this feuding shit has got to stop. It's bad for business, and when I say business, I mean *my* business and my money. And what happens when my money gets fucked up? I get angry, and none of you young mothafuckas wanna see me when I'm fuckin' angry! I don't know what's wrong with this new generation, but that's not how we handled shit back in my fuckin' day, you hear me? It's not how your parents would've handled it either."

"So what do you want from us?" Dallas asked.

"I want you to call a truce. You've both taken an eye for an eye. It's done. If it doesn't involve business, let it fucking go before the feds rain down on all of us," Al said.

Dallas looked at me, and I looked right back at him.

"Fine. We're in as long as these pussy ass niggas agree to stay the fuck on their side of Miami."

"Bitch nigga, we own Miami," I told him.

"A bitch is what you call that fine ass fiancée of yours, and I ain't no female, nigga," he replied.

"A bitch can be a female or a male... just like a ho. If that's what you actin' like, that's what the fuck I'm going to call you," I told him.

"Yeah, Darius, you better let your bitch ass brother know we'll slap a pussy nigga if he act out, and that's on my fuckin' brother," Blaze added.

"Nigga, I'm not gon' sit here and let you ho me. You got somethin' you feel like you need to get off your fuckin' chest, then say that shit and we can handle the shit right now," Dallas said, standing up.

"If you thinkin' I'm gon' back down, you got the wrong nigga, mothafucka!" I said, standing up as well.

Nothing stood in between us but the table and opportunity. I could feel my blood pressure rising by the second. My pride would always be stronger than any emotion inside me. Dallas knew not to fuck with me the way he was. Talkin' all that slick shit out his mouth wasn't going to do anything but get his ass fucked up. It was one thing to talk shit, but he wasn't about to keep bringing my girl into it. I was ready to show him why they called me Law.

"Nigga, I know for a fact your bitch pussy get wet for me, so if

95

you don't want her fucked, keep her ass from around me. You feel me?" He snickered.

At that point, I was done talking and done trying to be the only levelheaded mothafucka in the room. Before I could jump across the table and beat his ass, Blaze let a single gunshot ring through the air. People in the front of the club started screaming and running for cover.

"Bitch nigga, I've caught a case before, and I'll do it again. You think I'm scared to pull this fuckin' trigger? Huh?" Blaze asked, pointing the gun straight at Dallas.

"Let's go!" I said, pulling at Blaze's stiff arm.

He still had his gun aimed at Dallas for talking shit and disrespecting me and Shiya. Part of me wanted him to pull the trigger, but I knew it wouldn't do anything but start the very war that Alastair was trying to prevent. Those Price niggas were just tryna come up. That was the only reason they hated us the way they did. These niggas were praying on the downfall of the Calloway name, but it wasn't going to fuckin' happen.

* * *

Blaze

I was still so pissed off at them niggas that my blood was boiling. I knew better than to sit down with their asses in the first place. Law might've been on some kumbaya shit, but I knew nothing good was going to come from meeting with their asses, and I was right, too.

"Why the fuck you ain't let me shoot both of they asses? All our problems would've been solved!" I yelled as I banged on the dashboard with the palms of my hands.

"Too many fuckin' witnesses, nigga! You gotta start thinking with your fucking brain instead of those bullets all the fuckin' time," he told me. "You always ready to start somethin' that you might not be able to finish."

"Might not be able to finish? When the fuck have I ever started somethin' I couldn't finish, huh? Let me know that shit right now, nigga."

"I'm not about to sit here and go back and forth with your ass, Blaze."

"Exactly. Because you don't know a time, nigga."

"You remember when you were like fifteen and you had broken into that old white man's car down at the mall and took it joyriding?"

"Yeah. What about it?"

"You remember when his ass kept threatening to call the police and you ain't want to go back to juvie? So, what did you do, huh? You called me and Wolfe to come bail your ass out."

"Okay, that was one damn time, yo. All y'all did was beat his fuckin' ass and tell him if he..."

"If he called the cops, we would fuckin' kill him," he said, finishing my sentence.

"Yeah. Exactly. I could've did that myself."

"Nah, you were too busy showin' off, tryna make a name for yourself and not to be the baby anymore. That's all that was."

"And you ain't never wanna make a name for yourself? You just ain't wake up one day and niggas started callin' you Law. You made a point to a nigga and showed 'em what's up, and that's how you earned your respect. That's all I wanted back then was some fuckin' respect," I told him.

Law nodded his head slowly.

"Yeah, I guess you're right. You know Wolfe was out there, following in dad's footsteps early. Then when he died, Wolfe just kinda assumed the position, you know? That's what happens when you grow up in a family with all boys. You just kind of fall into the shadows sometimes."

"So, how'd you break out of Wolfe's shadow?" I asked.

"I was at school one day. Wolfe was home sick or somethin'. Whatever it was, he wasn't there. I was in the cafeteria, and I over-heard some bum ass niggas talkin' shit out the side of they neck, you know? Real slick shit about Wolfe and how he thought he was that nigga all because of who our father was. They ain't think I was gon' say nothin', like I was scared or somethin' because Wolfe wasn't around, but nah, that's not how it went down. I walked up to them. It had to have been like three of them, but there was only one who was really talkin' shit. The other two were just sitting there nodding and laughing. So, I walked up to them like what's up? You got somethin' to say about my brother? The nigga stood up and so did his friends. He was Wolfe's age, and I was only a freshman, maybe a sophomore at the time. This nigga put his fuckin' pointer finger into my forehead, and I lost it. I flipped my lunch tray over to dump all my food off and smacked his ass clear across the face with it. Boom!"

"Oh shit. After all these years, why have I never heard this fuckin' story?" I asked.

"I don't know. Maybe you never felt the need to ask until now."

"What else happened? I know his bitch ass boys probably tried to jump in, right?"

"Nah. They didn't actually. I smacked their bitch ass friend so hard that I knocked a few of his teeth clear out his mouth. When his ass hit the floor, I kept beating him until three teachers and a security guard finally got me off him, still kicking and punching. I damn near got kicked out of school for the rest of the year for that shit. But when I did go back, that's when niggas started callin' me

Law. They said I would break the law for my family and beat the shit out of any nigga that disrespected our name, which was true, so I stuck with it."

"Yeah, nigga. You ain't never tell me no story like that before. All this time I just thought it was some shit that you made up one day or somethin." I chuckled.

"Nah. Never that. You don't get respect by fakin' out here. You know that."

"Yeah, I do."

I turned my attention out of the window as Law and I rode in silence for a few minutes until I realized something.

"Yo, what's tomorrow's date?"

"The 27th," he told me.

"Ain't tomorrow your birthday?" I asked.

"Yeah." He nodded.

"Oh shit. What the fuck, nigga? Why ain't you hype about it?"

"When you start getting older, you start to see every day on this Earth as a birthday. Real talk."

"Aw, damn all that philosophical bullshit, nigga. You about to be twenty-eight. It's gonna be lit! What we doin'? Where we goin' tomorrow? Shit, with all that just went down, I could use the release," I told him.

"I hadn't put much thought into it at all." He shrugged.

I shook my head. Law was a real Debbie Downer-ass nigga sometimes. I respected him because he made sure damn near every move he made was calculated, and he watched my back like a second shadow, but I still wanted him to take a walk on the wild side with me every once in a while and live a little, especially before he married Nashiya's ass.

"You know what? Say no more. I got you. You just make sure your ass is ready to turn up with me!"

* * *

Raquel

I was really going stir crazy just sitting in the house. I hadn't gotten out since going with Law to that beautiful yacht. I was still pissed off at Law and avoided him any chance I could after our last encounter. Not that he noticed because he had been avoiding me, too. All I was trying to do was be honest with him, and if he couldn't take that, then his sensitive ass should've never came to talk to me in the first place.

The knock on my door snapped me out of my trance, and I got up to open it. Blaze was standing on the other side with a pair of jeans on, no shirt, three gold chains around his neck, and a pinky ring with four rows of diamonds on it, smiling.

"Aren't you sparkling," I told him.

Blaze chuckled.

"I know, right? What are you doing?"

"Oh, you know me... a little of this and a little of that, which really means a whole lot of nothing."

"Damn, that bored, huh?"

"Yeah, that bored." I nodded.

"Come out with us tonight then to celebrate Law's birthday."

"Uh, no. I don't think so."

"Why not?"

"Well, for one, your brother's fiancée hates me. Two, I don't think your brother is too fond of me right now either." I sighed.

"What happened between y'all two?"

"What do you mean what happened? Nothing happened. We just had a... a misunderstanding. That's all."

Blaze stroked his chin and looked me up and down.

"Listen, Raquel, I don't know what this misunderstanding was about, but Law is a real nigga, and Shiya is a real bitch, emphasis on the bitch, but you ain't hear that from me. If you can't fuck with that, then just leave it alone. I'm serious. You don't want to get tied up in that. Shiya might be bougie as hell, but she'll beat your little ass. You're better off sticking with me."

"You?" I asked.

"Yeah, me. You know you think I'm cute," he said, flashing me another wide smile.

"Yeah, so?"

"So, I think you're cute too, and I think you should let me take you out some time."

"On a date?"

"Uh, yeah. I guess if you wanna call it that." He shrugged.

"What else would I call it?"

"I don't know... I don't think I've ever been out on a real date before. I'm more of a Netflix and fuck type of guy."

"Don't you mean Netflix and chill?" I asked.

"Nah." He chuckled. "I meant exactly what I said."

"Wow... Thanks for the honesty I guess," I said, with my face screwed up.

"So, you comin' out tonight or what?"

"Yeah, sure, I'll go."

"Cool. Go on and get dressed then. We're leaving for KOD in an hour."

"Wait. What's KOD?"

Blaze looked at me and shook his head.

"Damn, girl. You really don't know shit about Miami, do you? KOD is King of Diamonds. You know... the strip club."

"Oh, yeah. Okay. Got it!" I nodded.

Blaze walked back down the hallway, and I shook my head. He really was a piece of work. I got dressed and let my natural curls flow down my back. I came downstairs and stood beside Blaze, who was standing by the door fixing the cufflinks on his crisp, white button-up shirt that he neglected to actually button.

"What is she doing here?" Nashiya asked.

"I invited her. She's with me," Blaze told her.

Nashiya looked me up and down and then rolled her eyes as she walked outside. I turned my attention to the top of the stairs where Law was standing. The two of us locked eyes as he made his way down, but neither of us spoke. He just walked past me and headed outside, too.

"Don't worry about them. Just c'mon," Blaze told me as he grabbed my hand.

The four of us got into a black SUV and rode in silence, letting the music be the only noise inside the car. I watched as Nashiya held Law's right hand as he drove with his left, and rolled my eyes. I decided if I was going to make it through the night without vomiting, I was going to have to direct my attention elsewhere.

We pulled up to the strip club that looked more like a large, blue warehouse on the outside with neon lighting. Blaze and I got out first, while Nashiya and Law took their time. I followed Blaze up to the front and the host led the four of us to a private VIP section. We walked through the sea of people crowding around all of the strippers, and I couldn't take my eyes off them. There were women in there defying gravity by hanging from the ceiling, doing handstands while wearing six-inch heels, and twirling around the poles like naked ballerinas.

After we were seated, four bottle girls came over to us with sparkling bottles of liquor and placed them in front of us. An array of strippers soon followed, and Blaze pulled out a wad of cash and started making it rain like Christmas had come early. The girls started twerking hard for their money, and I couldn't knock them. There were girls walking around there with two or three trash bags full of money. Seeing that really made me start to second guess my decision of going to college. There I was in student loan debt up to my elbows while those girls were walking around with enough cash to pay four years of my college tuition and then some.

"Do you want something to drink?" Blaze asked, as he held a bottle of Moët in his hand.

"Yeah, sure." I nodded.

"Open your mouth."

"What?"

"Just trust me."

I tilted my head back and opened my mouth wide as Blaze poured the champagne straight from the bottle. I swallowed it all in one gulp, and the two of us laughed.

"See. That wasn't so bad, was it?"

"No, not as bad as I thought it was going to be," I said, wiping the corners of my mouth.

"C'mon. Let's dance," he said as he grabbed my hand. "Let me see what you're working with."

"You want me to dance on you at a strip club? Ain't that their job?" I asked, pointing to all the strippers crowding around our section.

"That's exactly what I want," he whispered in my ear as he gently brushed his lips against my neck.

Ian

I was going crazy watching Blaze and Raquel together while Nashiya sat beside me eating it all up. I knew he was too much for her, and he wouldn't do shit but break her heart. Blaze had shown time and time again that he wasn't going to be tamed by any woman. He wasn't a beast that Raquel needed to rumble with.

"Happy birthday, baby," Nashiya said, snapping me out of my trance.

"Thank you."

"Are you enjoying yourself?"

"Um, yeah. I would've been cool with stayin' in the house with you, but it's cool. I haven't been to KOD in a minute."

Nashiya nodded and then looked over at Blaze and Raquel. My eyes followed hers.

"Looks like those two are really hitting it off, huh?"

"I guess." I shrugged.

"Is something wrong?"

"Nah. Nothing's wrong."

"So, how about we get out of here and uh... I'll give you some birthday head on the way back to the house, baby. I know that'll put a smile on that sexy face." She smiled.

"What about them?"

"Blaze is a big boy. He can take care of himself, and she looks to be enjoying his company, so what's the problem?"

"Ain't no problem. C'mon. Let's go then," I said as I stood and grabbed her hand.

I walked over to Blaze, who was still all wrapped up in Raquel and the strippers, and tapped him on the shoulder. He turned around with his chest out and poured some champagne down his chest while the strippers took turns licking it off.

"What's up, birthday boy?" he asked as he threw his arm around my shoulder. "You enjoying yourself?"

"Yeah, it's cool. Thank you, but uh, me and Shiya are about to head home."

"Head home? Y'all can't leave yet. They haven't even brought your cake out."

"Cake?"

"Yeah, nigga. Just sit tight for a second and throw these so you can pay for one of these ho's college tuition," he said, handing me a band of money.

"Whatever." I chuckled, brushing his wild ass off.

"Back to these hos! They callin me!" he said as he walked off with a new bottle of Moët attached to his hand.

I shook my head at my little brother and turned to face Nashiya.

"We're staying a little while longer, bae."

A little while longer turned into four more hours. The night soon became a blur. All I remembered were numerous rounds of shots, smacking stripper asses, and trying to keep my mind and eyes off Raquel. The four of us walked out of the club and stumbled to the car. I started the engine and focused on getting us home safely. Nashiya had passed out in the passenger seat, and all I heard was Blaze mumbling in Raquel's ear and her giggling. I gripped the steering wheel tighter and pressed the gas a little harder. As soon as we got home, I carried Nashiya to our room and put her in the bed. I took my shirt off and kept my wife beater on. I knew I should've just laid down beside Shiya and went to bed, but I couldn't get Raquel and Blaze off my mind.

I closed my bedroom door behind me, walked down to

Raquel's room, and knocked gently on the door. She opened the door wearing a tank top and a pair of very small shorts.

"Hey." I said.

"Hey. Happy belated birthday..."

"Thank you.." I nodded.

"Did you want something? I was about to go to sleep," she said, pointing back at the bed.

"You got something going on with my brother?" I blurted out.

I made an effort to look past her and into the room to see if Blaze had crept his way inside.

"And if I did, would that be any of your business?" she asked, folding her arms across her chest so I wouldn't see her nipples getting hard from the breeze of the A/C.

"I don't know what's up with the two of y'all, but you looked real comfortable with one another tonight. He's my baby brother, and I love him, but Blaze is a different type of nigga. He ain't like them preppy college boys you're probably used to, aight? He acts like showing love to a female or loving a female in general is against the law or somethin'. That's just that young nigga mentality he got, and I just... I don't wanna see you gettin' hurt or nothin' like that..."

"Don't you think that's for me to decide? Maybe I don't want love. Maybe I just want to do like you said and get losing my virginity over with."

I clenched my jaw and grinded my teeth for a second before I responded.

"Look, all I'm saying is Blaze is the type of nigga who will break your heart and blow the pieces right back in your face. I've seen it too many times. He's too wild and reckless for you, Raquel."

"Thanks for the advice, but I never had any intention on fucking him or doing anything with him. He tried and I politely shut his ass down, so if you don't mind, I'd like to go to sleep now. Oh, and Law, if you want me to mind my business, how about you do the same and let me 'play my role' in peace," she said with air quotes.

"Are you still upset about that?"

"I'm fine, Law," she said, shaking her head.

"Look, I'm sorry about what I said. I was having a bad night, and the shit you were saying was getting to me. That's all."

"Why? Because it was the truth? Oh, I get it. You want me to lie to you like the rest of these niggas."

"Watch your mouth, Raquel."

"Whatever. Lie to me all you want, but you can't lie to your reflection in the damn mirror, Law. Besides, I didn't ask you to come in here. I didn't ask you to stand up for me. I didn't ask to you do any of that shit!"

"You didn't have to."

"What do you mean?" she asked.

"I mean, I can tell how I make you feel just by looking at you. I notice everything about people. I always have."

"And?"

"And, I can tell you're attracted to me. You're just too stubborn to say it."

"Well, I think your body language radar is way off because I don't want you. Do you know what I want? What I really, *really* want?"

"What's that?" I asked.

"I want to be over and done with this bullshit. I want to go the fuck home. I want to get as fucking far away from Miami as possible so I never have to see your ass again!" she yelled.

I sighed and shut the door behind me, stepping closer to her.

"Lower your voice, aight? Look, I can't let you go until I know the cops are going to close the case about that hotel shit, aight? If they find you, they find me, and I can't have that shit. So just sit tight."

"Whatever, Law. Just get out of my room."

I could see tears welling up in the corners of her eyes and

immediately felt bad. All I had been trying to do was look out for her, but my words just never seemed to come out right.

"Raquel, I'm sorry, okay? You're right. What you do with my brother or any other nigga has nothing to do with me. I'll leave you alone."

"That's the smartest thing you've said to me all night," she said, folding her arms across her chest even tighter.

Her stance and the way her nostrils flared was turning me on. Although I knew better, something inside me was telling me to tell her how I really felt about her.

"I just want to know one thing..."

"What?"

"Are you seriously thinking about letting my brother take your virginity?"

"What? No. Didn't I just tell you I had no intentions of fucking him? He's far from my type anyway."

"What is your type again, Raquel?"

"It doesn't matter," she said, shaking her head.

"I think it does," I said, as I closed in the space between us.

"What are you doing?"

"I'm waiting until you tell me what your type is because I don't think you been fuckin' with the right type of niggas."

"And what exactly does that mean?"

"You been out here fuckin' with these college boys your whole life who don't know shit but books. What can he bring to the table that you don't already know? You need a nigga that can teach you about some shit you can't learn from no stuck-up college professor and shit."

"A nigga like you?" she asked boldly.

"Yeah, exactly. You need a nigga like me, Raquel. I know for a fact that you never been with no real hitta."

* * *

Raquel

I couldn't believe what I was hearing, and thought for sure it must've been the drinks I had earlier talking. I knew I needed to respond, and I needed to respond quickly, but I was at a loss for what to say.

"Well, I can't have a nigga like you because your girl is here and very much in love!"

Law cut his eyes at me. Before I could get another word out, he stepped closer to me and kissed me. His lips were warm pressed against mine. I could feel myself floating away almost. He grabbed the sides of my face and kissed my deeper, slowly sliding his tongue into my mouth. It felt too damn good to stop until he did.

"I'm sorry. I shouldn't have done that," he admitted. "It was a mistake."

I wiped my bottom lip and nodded, trying to regain my footing and slow my heartrate back down.

"Yeah, I know. You're right."

I stared into Law's eyes. I hated the way he looked at me. It made me melt every single time. I could've easily drowned in his eyes. Everyone was afraid of him. I could see how cowardly they were around him when he walked past. His demeanor demanded power, but I wasn't afraid. I was intrigued. A part of me wanted him to take me right there and drive our bodies into one another like a car crash. He stepped closer to me again until his lips brushed against mine. I could feel his breath fan across my face. My knees were flimsy like a piece of loose-leaf paper in the wind as I stood waiting for him to make another move, but he didn't.

"Goodnight," he said instead.

I exhaled without even realizing I'd been holding my breath during the entirety of our stare down.

"Goodnight, Law."

After he closed the door behind him, I stood there for a moment, frozen in my step. I'd always been a fan of kissing. There was something romantic to me about the way the lips of two people could connect and say so much without saying actual words. But what Law and I had shared was different. I wanted him from the top of his head to the soles of his feet. I walked into the bathroom and looked at my reflection in the mirror. My face was flushed pink, my heart was still racing out of my chest, and I swear I saw lovebirds floating around my head. That's when I knew what I'd been trying to avoid thinking about since I first laid eyes on him. I wanted Law to take my virginity.

CHAPTER ELEVEN

Law

I laid awake all night replaying the kiss in my head. Just thinking about how soft Raquel's lips felt made me anxious to know how the rest of her body felt and tasted. I couldn't hide the fact that I wanted to dig in Raquel's pussy like I was gettin' outta lock up. A part of me did feel bad, though. I'd never been a cheater, but I was glad I knew what Raquel's lips felt like. I knew I needed to stay away from her, but my body was drawing me nearer to her day by day. I hated having the thoughts I was having because Shiya had been nothing but loyal to me from day one.

Shiya rolled over and wrapped her arms around me. I held her close to me and kissed the top of her forehead. I had to remember to keep my eye on the prize, and that prize was Shiya. The more I laid there, the guiltier I felt. I gently slid Shiya's sleeping body off me and rolled her over onto her back. I slid underneath the covers and lifted the dress that she was still wearing from the club. I wasn't surprised that she didn't have any panties on. She never liked to wear them anyway.

"Law," she moaned. "Baby, what are you doing?"

"I'm sorry, baby," I mumbled into her pussy as I kissed it.

I reached up, grabbed her left breast through her dress, and gave it a tight squeeze. She moaned a little louder. I could tell she was waking up and getting more into the moment. I laid on my stomach and licked her smooth pussy in short, quick circles. She sat up on her elbows and watched me. I put my left hand on the top of her pussy to spread her lips so that my tongue could go deep inside her.

"Mmm. Shit, baby," she said as she gripped the back of my head as I continued to flick her clit with my tongue.

She put her cold feet on my bare back and rubbed them up and down my spine. Nashiya popped her breasts out of the top of her dress and gave her nipples a tight squeeze as I sucked on her clit.

"Oooh yeah, baby. Just like that. Eat that fuckin' pussy, baby."

Nashiya held her legs up by her head and spread her legs for me as I licked deeper. Her shallow breathing told me she was near her climax. I started writing my name with my tongue on her pussy, which made her squirm and palm the sides of my head, forcing me to stay still.

"Ohhh shit, Law!" She squealed. "I'm cumming, baby! I'm fucking cumming!"

Her body jolted forward, and she put her hand in between my mouth and her pussy as she came. Her skin was glistening with a mixture of my spit and her juices. I sucked her fingers slowly.

"Mmm. That's my girl," I told her.

Nashiya

Law woke me up in the most beautiful way. I wished I could've woke up like that every single morning. As much as I wanted to lay, wrapped up in our bedsheets all day, I had business to handle. I crawled out of bed and headed straight for the shower. Once I got myself together, I grabbed my keys, cell phone, and purse.

"Where are you running off to in such a hurry?" Law asked.

"Oh, baby, I didn't tell you? I'm going to meet Janique for a little girl time. You know? We might grab a bite to eat and hit a couple stores so I can find something sexy to wear for you on our honeymoon."

"I think I like it best when you wear nothing at all." He smirked.

I flashed him a smile and winked at him.

"Later, baby. I love you."

"I love you, too."

A part of me hated lying to Law, but I knew it was for his own good. Yeah, Blaze had tried his hand at wooing Raquel, but I knew he was too fickle to really make a commitment, so I called in reinforcements. I pulled up to Big Pink down on the strip and parked my car. I sat outside on the restaurant's patio, staring down at the menu until my guest arrived.

"Well, look who we have here," Dallas said as he walked up to my table and peered at me over the top of his sunglasses.

I stood to greet him with a hug.

"I'm glad you could make it."

"Mmmmmm," he said, licking his lips. "How could I turn down a call from the love of my life? You still look as good as ever, too."

"Thank you." I nodded.

"What have you been up to besides scheming and scamming?" he asked.

"Chill out with that, aight? I don't do that shit no more. I'm engaged to be married now."

"Oh, trust me, I heard all about your little engagement. Does your bitch ass fiancé know I used to fuck you from sun up to sundown?"

I rolled my eyes.

"Lower your fucking voice, aight? And, no. He doesn't, and I plan to keep it that way at least until after the wedding."

"Mmhm, your ol' scheming ass. What do they say? You can take the girl out the hood, but you can't take the hood out the girl, right?"

"Look, I called you here because I need you to do something for me."

"If it has anything to do with taking one of them Calloway niggas out, my hands are tied right now. Business reasons," he said.

"It's not about that. I would never ask you to do that."

"Then what is it about?"

I pulled out my phone and showed him a picture of Raquel from her Facebook page.

"Yo, I know her," he said, pointing to the phone.

"How do you know her?"

"That's the shorty I met at the club at least a couple months ago. What she still doin' out here?"

"Don't worry about all that. It's a long story. Are you in or not?"

"You gon' have to tell me a little more information than that if you want me to stick my neck out of you while you're still sleeping with the enemy, Bird."

"What did I tell you about calling me that?" I snapped.

"Oh, my bad. Your man don't know about your lil' nickname either, huh?"

"No, he doesn't. My past is just that—my past. Yeah, you were a part of it, but you're not my future. He is."

"Fine," he said, raising his hands.

I leaned in closer to him and looked him in his eyes.

"What if I told you that the girl in this picture could help your family in more ways than one?"

"I'm listening."

"She was there the night your brother Damien was murdered at that hotel."

"What the fuck did you just say?"

"No. No more. That's all you get. Are you in or are you fucking out? I need to get this bitch as far away from me and mine as possible."

Dallas looked at me for a second and nodded.

"What do you need me to do?"

"I just need you to be you, baby, just charming ol' you. That's all. Let me handle the rest. I'll be in touch later."

After my meeting with Dallas, I headed back to the house and went straight to Raquel's room and knocked.

"Hey. You got a second?" I asked as soon as she opened the door.

"For the last time, Nashiya, I'm not fucking your man."

"I'm not here about that. I know that now. I actually came here to apologize."

"Apologize?" she asked.

"Yeah." I sighed. "I know I can come off as a bitch sometimes, and I don't know... Maybe all this wedding stuff has turned me into a bridezilla or something, but whatever the case may be, I wanted to apologize."

"Wow... That's really big of you."

"Do you accept it?" I asked.

"Um, yeah. Sure, I do."

"Cool. Maybe you and I could grab lunch or something tomorrow?" I asked. "I'm sure you want to get out of the house and get some fresh air, right?"

"Fresh air is always good." She nodded.

"Alright. Well, it's set. We'll do lunch tomorrow around noon-ish. Be ready by 11:30 a.m.," I told her and turned to leave.

As soon as I closed the door, I smiled. That bitch was almost too gullible for me to take her ass seriously. My plan was set in motion. Dallas was going to break that bitch down and have her so wrapped up in him that she wouldn't have time to notice Law anymore.

* * *

Raquel

"So, where do you want to eat?" Nashiya asked me as soon as she started the car.

"I don't know. Anywhere sounds good right about now. I'm starving," I told her.

"Hmm. What are you in the mood for? Anything particular? You want soul food, Italian, Mexican, or fast food?"

"Soul food sounds good."

"Okay. Great. I know just the spot."

I sat back as Nashiya drove us to Jackson Soul Food. After we ordered, we sat across from each other in silence.

"So the big day is coming up, huh?" I asked.

"Yeah, I can't wait. Three weeks and counting."

"Are you having a bachelorette party or anything?"

"Yeah. I'm sure my girls are going to throw me something. They can be pretty wild when they want to be." She chuckled.

"My friends are like that, too. They were always throwing me ideas for mine."

"Wait. You're married?" she asked, almost choking on her drink.

"Engaged. Well, at least I was before coming here."

"What happened if you don't mind me asking?"

"The night I graduated from college, I caught him fucking my roommate, who also happened to be my maid of honor," I said, shaking my head.

"Damn," she said shaking her head.

I chuckled.

"Yeah, that's pretty much everybody's reaction when I tell them."

"Excuse me, ladies," a man said as he walked over to our table.

"I don't mean to interrupt, but don't I know you?" he said, turning his attention to me.

I looked up at him and immediately recognized him as the guy I'd met in the club when I first got down to Miami.

"Uh... yeah. I think we met once."

"At the club, right?"

"Yeah, the club," I nodded.

"Excuse me. Where are my manners? Hi. I'm Dallas," he said, shaking Nashiya's hand.

"Shiya. Nice to meet you." She smiled.

Dallas turned back to me and smiled.

"So back to you, miss. I called you."

"Did you?"

"I really thought you played me that night after the club."

"Nah. It wasn't like that. I actually uh... ended up losing my phone the next day, so I never got it. I'm sorry."

"Well, let me reintroduce myself and start over. How about that?"

"Sure." I giggled.

"I'm Dallas Price, and it's very nice to make your acquaintance again, beautiful."

"Well it's nice to meet you again, Dallas. I'm Raquel," I said, shaking his hand.

"Would it be possible for me to give you my number again, Raquel? Maybe this time you won't slip off into the night like Cinderella and leave me heartbroken for a second time." He chuckled. "Was that corny?"

"It was, but I liked it." I smiled.

"Good, because I would like to take you out to dinner, and I don't know... catch up or somethin'."

"I uh... don't have a phone right now," I admitted.

"Well, whenever you get a new one, give me a call, beautiful."

I watched Dallas write his number down on a napkin and hand it to me.

"Thanks."

"Oh, and before you ask, the offer for you being my woman is still on the table." He smiled.

"Okay. I'll remember that." I smiled.

"You ladies enjoy your lunch. Raquel, I hope I'll be seeing you soon."

As soon as Dallas was out of earshot, I looked at Nashiya, who was grinning from ear to ear.

"Whhhaattt?" I said, drawing out the word.

"Nothing." She smiled. "He was fine as hell, girl."

"I know, right?" I smiled.

"We need to get you a phone."

"For what?"

"How else you gon' call him?"

"Oh." I nodded.

"I mean, unless you're not interested, which to me means either you're a low-key lesbian or you're interested in someone else, so which one is it?" she questioned.

"I am interested." I nodded. "I just haven't dated in a very long time."

"Oh, well nothing fails but a try. You gotta get back out there some time, right?"

I nodded, knowing she was right. Plus, I was excited at the possibility of getting a phone. That to me sounded like I was one step closer to my ticket out of Miami for good.

CHAPTER TWELVE

Raquel

s much as I wanted to be happy that I'd seen Dallas
again, I couldn't get Law and the kiss we shared off my
mind. I knew he'd been avoiding me yet again, which
made me feel even worse. I at least thought we would be able to
talk about it like adults instead of avoiding each other once again
like the plague.

Nashiya had gotten me a new iPhone and told me not to tell
Law. I didn't trust her as far as I could throw her, but I wasn't
going to not accept it. As soon as I got my phone, I went into the
bathroom and called Camille. I had already prepared myself for a
cuss out.

"Hello?" she answered.

"Cam..."

"Oh my God, Raquel. Is that you?" She squealed into the
receiver.

Her scream was loud. I pulled the phone away from my ear
and turned the volume down.

"Yes. It's me," I assured her.

"Where in the *fuck* have you been?"

"I know I have a lot of explaining to do."

"You damn right you do," she said, cutting me off.

"Okay, okay, listen. You know I went through a lot with that whole Derrick shit, and I just... I just needed to get away and start over, you know? So, I made a conscious but rash decision to stay out here for a while. I got a job and everything."

"You what?"

"Just tell me you're happy for me, please."

"That's the thing, Raqi, I don't know if I'm happy for you yet. I haven't seen or heard from you in almost two months."

"I know and I'm sorry. I lost my phone, and I'm just now saving up enough money to get a new one, but if it makes you feel any better, you're the first person I called." I smiled.

"Mmhm, whatever."

"And... and I might be coming home soon... you know... to visit."

"To visit, huh?" she asked skeptically.

"Yes."

"And what about that boy you were down there with? Is he coming with you for this so-called visit?"

"I don't know. He might."

"Derrick would probably have a heart attack if he saw you with someone new."

"Fuck Derrick! I don't give a fuck what he thinks!"

"Then I guess you don't want to know that he keeps asking me about you any and every chance he gets."

I paused for a second and then chewed my bottom lip.

"What'd he say?"

"The usual. He wants me to tell you how much he misses you, and he knows he fucked up. All that rah rah, blah blah mess."

"Bullshit basically."

"Exactly," she agreed.

"Enough about his ass... I miss you."

"Are you sure you're okay, Raquel? This is my last time asking."

"Yeah. I'm fine. I'm just adjusting still. That's all. It's like when I went off to college and was depressed for the first month, but then I got into the swing of things and I was fine."

"Girl, yes. I get it, but I told you to get some, not fall in love and run off with the man in a whole new state!" Camille chuckled.

"I know, right?" I nodded.

Camille's voice sounded like home. Talking to her was the only thing that kept me sane in my mind-numbing situation.

"Well, I gotta go. I just wanted to call and hear your voice. I'll talk to you soon, okay?"

"Okay, girl. I love you."

"I love you, too."

I ended the call and held the phone to my chest. To avoid crying, I decided to go back in my room and watch TV to clear my mind. I put the phone on silent and hid it underneath my bed. I woke up later that night to a growling stomach. I pulled the phone out to check the time. It was after 1:00 a.m. I put the phone back and headed downstairs to the kitchen. To my surprise, Law was down there.

"Hey..." I said, awkwardly.

"Hey, Raquel."

"I was just coming to grab something to snack on, but I'll come back later," I said as I turned on my heels.

"Raquel, wait. I thought about what you said the other night."

"And?" I asked, resting my elbows on the island in the middle of the kitchen floor.

"And I think you're right..."

"You can't just stir up all these feelings inside me and then leave me open to deal with them alone. That's not how it works, Law."

"That's where you're wrong. That's exactly how this works. I want you, Raquel, but I need to stay the fuck away from you, and I can't. I don't fucking want to. Every time I see you, I think about bending your fucking ass over, spreading those pussy lips, and sliding my dick right up in between those thighs of yours. That shit drives me fucking crazy! You had me ready to fight my brother, my own fuckin' blood over you!"

I walked around the island and stood in front of him.

"Fuck me, Law," I said boldly.

"Stop saying shit you don't mean, Raquel, I swear to God," he said, stepping closer to me.

"I'm serious. I want you to fuck me. Right now."

Law scooped me up into his arms and sat me on the edge of the island. He put his lips on mine, and it was as if electricity jolted throughout my entire body. He ran his hands up my smooth thighs and continued to kiss me gently. As soon as he spread my legs, I could feel my panties start to flood. Law rubbed on my pussy through my panties and then slid them to the side and fingered me slowly. I loved how he touched me.

"Mmm, shit. You're so wet already."

Law lowered himself in front of my pussy and pulled my shorts and my soaking wet panties off. As soon as his tongue touched my sensitive clit, I squirmed as my back arched. He kissed my inner thigh and then flicked his tongue against my clit once more. I reached down to rub his head as he licked from the top of my pussy to my asshole. Law slowly ran his tongue in circles against my soft pussy lips as he held on tight to my waist.

I sat up on my elbows and threw my head back as I arched my back some more to put my pussy right on his face. I rubbed my nipples through my shirt as I watched him. He was so fucking sexy.

"Mmm. Taste how sweet you are," he said as he kissed me and swirled his tongue around inside my mouth.

He pulled me down off the island and turned me around so that my back was facing him. He rubbed his hard dick against the crack of my ass through his boxers.

"I want to fuck you so bad." He breathed into the nape of my neck.

"Then do it, Law. Fuck me." I groaned.

"You don't mean that."

"I mean it. I want you to take my virginity," I said as I turned around to look him in his eyes.

"Not here," he said, looking around.

Law picked me up and carried me down the hallway into his office. He didn't even bother to turn the lights on. He pushed everything off the desk and sat me on it. He pulled my shirt up over my head and ran his large hands over my natural C-cup breasts. I laid my back against the cold wood surface and watched him as he sucked on my breasts while massaging my thighs. He looked up at me and kissed me passionately, pulling down his shorts.

"Do you want it?"

I nodded.

"I do."

"Then show me."

"What do you want me to do?"

"If you want the dick, pull it out."

I reached my hand down and ran my hand over his hard dick that was still inside his boxers. Then I put my hand inside and pulled it out over the top of the elastic band. Law pulled his boxers down and stood in front of me in all of his glory. He was beautiful and so was his dick. I put my hand back on his dick and moved my hand up and down his shaft. It was a nice size, much bigger than Derrick's was, so I knew it was going to hurt much worse.

Law slid his finger inside me again, and I instantly felt myself about to cum. He moved his middle finger in and out. After he made sure my pussy was nice and wet, he slid the tip of his dick inside me. My back arched, and I gasped. The pain was excruciating.

"Ooooh..." I groaned.

"Let me know if you want me to stop, Raquel."

"No, no, I want you to keep going."

Law continued to slowly push inside me. I dug my nails into his back until the pain subsided. He kissed me to try and take my mind off the discomfort. After a few slow strokes, it started to feel better, and my body started to relax.

"Goddamn, your pussy is so fuckin' tight." He groaned through clenched teeth.

He reached underneath me to grab my ass so that he could go deeper inside me.

"Mmm. Oh my God. This is so crazy."

"What do you mean?"

"I can't believe I'm doing this."

"We don't have to. We can stop right now if you want."

"No, no. I want to keep going. You feel so good."

As soon as those words fell off my lips, his phone began to vibrate in his shorts pocket on the floor next to his feet. He kept stroking inside me, ignoring the call. When the phone kept vibrating repeatedly, I stopped him.

"Maybe you should answer it."

Law kissed me and shook his head.

"Fuck that phone, Raquel."

The deeper he thrusted into me, the better it felt. I could feel myself nearing my climax and the feeling was almost uncontrollable.

"Ooooh shiiiiiitttttt," I said as I gripped Law's shoulders for dear life.

"Mmm. You cumming, Raquel? Huh? You cumming all over this dick?" he whispered in my ear.

"Yesss, Law. I'm cumming!" I screamed.

Law pumped inside me for a few more minutes before he slid out and came inside his hand.

After we were done, Law went to the bathroom to clean himself up and brought me a warm rag.

"Are you okay?" he asked.

"Never better," I assured him.

When the both of us were clean and redressed, he flipping on the lights and pulled out his cell phone.

"Yo, Blaze. What's up?"

"Where have you been, Law? I've been blowing you up, nigga! What the fuck have you been doing?"

"I was handling some business," he said as he looked over at me and kissed my forehead.

"I got some bad news for you, bruh."

"What?"

"It's about Shiya... She was in a bad car accident."

CHAPTER THIRTEEN

Nashiya

I laid in my hospital bed with all sorts of devices connected to me. Everyone, including the doctors were so happy that I'd survived my car accident with only a few bruises and a broken wrist. What they didn't know was that I'd cut my own brakes and sent my car slamming into the guardrail on the side of the interstate near our house. I made sure to set it up perfectly, too. I had to do something to make sure all of Law's attention was on me while Dallas worked his magic with Raquel, and if that didn't work, when Law found the knife and hammer I'd hidden underneath her bed, he would wipe his hands with her stupid ass. If I had to take a few bumps and bruises to make sure of that that, that was fine with me.

When Law burst through the door to my room, I knew it was time for me to get my Oscar-worthy performance on. He rushed over to me and kissed my forehead.

"Baby, are you okay? I'm sorry I wasn't here sooner. I got caught up handling some business."

"Yeah, baby. I'm fine. The doctors said they don't know how I survived. My car flipped three times!"

"Did they say how it happened? Were you speeding or anything?" he asked.

"Law... baby... I think somebody cut my brakes."

"Are you fucking serious?" he yelled.

"Baby, calm down, but yes, that's what I overheard the paramedics saying when they put me in the ambulance."

"Tell me everything you remember."

"Well, I was... I was leaving from Janique's house, and I was on my way home. I got in the car and started it like usual and backed out of my parking spot. I noticed my brakes were acting a little funny, but I figured I could make it home because you know she doesn't live that far away. As soon as it hit the interstate, I sped up, and when I tried to press the brake, it automatically went all the way down to the floor. I... I didn't know what to do, baby. I steered the car and kept hitting the brake, but nothing happened. So I... I unhooked my seatbelt, and I jumped out of the car. I watched it slam into the guardrail and then flip three times before landing on its head. I was so scared," I told him.

"Oh my God, baby. Come here," he said, taking me into his arms. "Everything is going to be okay, baby. I promise you that. I'm going to find out who did this shit."

"To be honest, baby, I think I already know who did it."

"Who?"

"Raquel... I tried apologizing to her a few days ago, and she wouldn't accept it. She damn near cussed me out and told me that I didn't deserve you and I deserved to die. I really think she might've had something to do with this."

"What? Your accident?"

"Yeah, my accident. The accident that could've fuckin' killed me, Law."

"C'mon now, Shiya. You know just as well as I do that Raquel isn't capable of doing anything malicious like that."

"You may not be able to see through her little innocent act, but I can, and I'm uncomfortable with her being in the house after all this. I don't trust her, baby," I said, wiping a tear.

"What do you want me to do, baby? Just let me know, and I'll do it."

"It's simple, Law. You either want me or her."

"You're right." He nodded. "I'm going to handle it, baby. Don't worry about it."

"I love you, Law," I told him as another tear slid down my cheek.

"I love you, too, baby, and I swear on my brother I'm going to get to the bottom of this and make sure whoever did this to you knows never to fuck with you or me again."

* * *

Raquel

I was laying on my bed in the dark, just reliving the moment Law and I had shared when there was a banging on my bedroom door that sent my heart racing.

"Open the mothafuckin' door, Raquel!" Law yelled on the other side.

"Law, what's wrong? Is everything okay?" I asked as soon as I opened the door.

I reached out for his arm, but he quickly snatched it away and walked past me into my room.

"Are you going to tell me what's going on? Is Nashiya okay?" I asked.

He ignored me and started rummaging through the drawers, slamming them shut and leaving some of them open. Then he dove under my bed.

"Law! Talk to me! Tell me what you're looking for. Maybe I can help!" I told him.

"She thinks you cut her brakes," he told me.

"Wait. What? Why would she think I did it? I don't know the first thing about cars, let alone how to cut somebody's fucking brakes!"

"Then what are these?" he asked, pulling out a knife and hammer from underneath my bed.

"Law... Wait. No. That's not mine!"

"And what's this, huh? A fucking phone? Who the fuck have you been talking to on a fucking phone, Raquel?"

"Whoa! Wait! Just calm down! I've never seen those tools a day in my life, Law. You've got to believe me! And the phone... Shiya got me that phone!"

Law threw the phone across the room, cracking the screen.

"Was this your fucking plan all along, huh? What? Come at me with your little virginity story and how your fiancé fucked your roommate, making me feel bad for you so you could try and kill my fiancée? And for what? You think I'd marry you instead? Is that what you think?"

I shook my head slowly as my facial expression crumbled up like a piece of paper. I couldn't believe the things that were coming out of his mouth. All I wanted to do was break down and cry, but my body was still in shock.

"This shit is too much! I don't need this fucking shit right now!" he yelled.

"I know this is stressful, but you've got to believe me. I didn't do this! I could never do something like that! You know that! You know me!"

"No. I don't know you, Raquel."

"Wh—what?" I said, choking back tears.

"Raquel, I need to get the fuck out of here."

"What? Law, y—you can't be serious. Are you serious right now?" I asked.

"I'm dead ass serious."

The cold look in his eyes solidified his statement.

"Wow... after we just... wow," I said, clenching my jaw.

"Look, I just can't deal with all this shit right now, Raquel. You've got to go."

"Really, Law? That's how you're going to do me?"

"I can't trust you, Raquel. Not now and maybe not ever."

"Me? You can't trust me? Fine. I'm done with all of this shit! I'm done with you, with that stupid bitch, and this whole shit. I hope you get exactly what's fucking coming to you, Law! I'm done!" I screamed as I threw my hands up in the air, grabbed the phone, and stormed out of the room.

CHAPTER FOURTEEN

Raquel

I didn't stop until I got out of the house. I could hear Law behind me, yelling my name, but I kept pushing forward. He deserved that lying ass bitch Nashiya and the miserable life he was going to have with her as his wife. If he couldn't see she was setting me up and was only around him for his money, he was dumber than he looked. I knew she was a ruthless ass bitch, but I never thought she'd try to frame me for trying to kill her. That was an all-time low even for someone like her.

"Raquel, wait up!" Blaze yelled as he ran up behind me and put his hand on my shoulder.

"Get the fuck off me!"

"Just hold up a second, aight? Calm down!"

"Calm down? You need to be telling your brother to calm down, not me!"

"Look, I heard the argument, and you're right. He's tripping."

I stopped walking and looked at Blaze.

"So you believe me?" I asked.

"Yeah, I do. I know you ain't like Shiya, but you ain't no killer, Raquel."

"If it's so easy for you to see, why is it so hard for your brother?"

"Law's just... He's just got a lot on his plate right now with the wedding and the family business and shit. All he wants to do is keep her happy right now. I promise you that's the only reason he's doing any of this."

"Yeah. Well, that don't make it right," I told him.

"Where are you going to go?"

"I don't know. I was going to figure it out as I went along. I just know I don't want to be here, and I don't want to see his mothafuckin' face ever again!" I yelled, hoping he'd hear me.

"Look, we have a penthouse down in South Beach. Wolfe used to do a lot of business over there. Let me take you there for the night until we figure some shit out, okay?"

I looked at him and nodded.

"Thank you."

Blaze and I got into his car and he sped off. After about 20 minutes or so, he pulled up to a high-rise building and put the car in park.

"Look, I've got to get back to the house and check on Law, but here's the key. It's penthouse number 872. The access code in the elevator is 1121," he told me.

"Ok... 1121. Got it," I told him.

"You sure you gon' be alright?"

"Yeah. I'll be fine. Thanks."

I got out of the car and made my way into the building. When I got up to the front door, I opened it and flipped on the light switch nearest to me. It was a big open space with shiny, tan marble floors. There were two Persian rugs in the living room underneath the tan leather furniture. Open windows covered all the walls, and I could see a clear view of the Atlantic Ocean's waves crashing into each other and flowing up the sand. There was also a grand piano sitting in the corner next to the dining room with a large chandelier.

I shoved the key in my pocket and laid down on the couch. I looked at the phone in my hand, which had a large crack in the screen, but it still worked for the most part. I logged into my iCloud account and let it download everything back to my phone. I scrolled through the app store and re-downloaded all of my old apps, too. It felt good not to have to hide the phone anymore, but I was still pissed off about how everything went down.

I sat the phone down, walked into the kitchen that had all stainless-steel appliances, and opened the refrigerator. There was nothing inside but a couple bottles of water. I pulled one out, cracked it open, and drank a swig before twisting the cap back on tight. I walked back into the living room and flopped back down on the couch all in my feelings. I just didn't understand how Law could go from making love to me to accusing me of trying to kill his fiancée. As much as I still cared for him, I'd lost all respect for him and that was something I wasn't sure if he'd ever be able to get back from me.

I went to my contacts and scrolled down until I saw Dallas's name. I hadn't called him since he'd given me his number at the soul food restaurant, but I needed a shoulder to lean on before I went bat shit crazy. I put the phone on speaker and waited for him to pick up.

"Hello?"

"Dallas?"

"Yeah. Who this?"

"Hey. It's me, Raquel..."

* * *

Ian

Ever since Raquel had moved out, my mood had been different and everybody, including Shiya knew it. I had no patience for anything or anybody, and it didn't take much to set me off. When Blaze told me that he had her staying in the penthouse apartment in South Beach, I was relieved. At least that way I knew where she was, and I could check on her if I needed to. Deep down I knew that there was no way Raquel was capable of doing anything like that to Shiya, but after what I'd done with her, I felt like I owed it to Shiya to make her feel comfortable, being that she was the woman of the house. Nashiya was home and recovering slowly. I was still relieved that she got away with just a few bumps, bruises, and a broken wrist. I would've felt ten times worse if she'd died while I was fucking Raquel. I didn't want things to be the way they were between us, and I knew I needed to apologize. Raquel was the type to wear all of her emotions on her sleeve, so I knew she probably hated me, and I didn't blame her.

I went over to the apartment and knocked a few times, and got no answer. I pulled my spare key out of my pocket and unlocked the door. The penthouse was pitch black.

"Raquel?" I yelled as I walked through the house, flipping on lights as I went.

I looked in every room for her and turned up empty.

"Where the fuck are you?" I mumbled to myself.

I sat down on the couch and decided to wait it out, figuring she may have went to take a walk on the beach or grab something to eat. She didn't have a car, so I knew she couldn't have went far. I quickly flipped the lights off when I heard keys jingling at the front door. I watched Raquel walk into the apartment, smiling from ear to ear like a little schoolgirl. She jumped when she turned the lights on and saw me standing in the living room.

"Law, what are you doing here?" she asked, grabbing her chest.

"Where have you been, Raquel?"

"What the fuck are you doing here?"

"Just answer my question. Where have you been?" I said calmly.

"I was out on a... I was out with a friend, okay?"

"What friend? Who have you been seeing?"

"Don't you have a fiancée to nurse back to health? You know? The one you think I tried to kill."

"Raquel, I didn't come here to argue, okay? Who have you been seeing?"

"Just this guy I met."

"What's his name?"

"I'm not telling you shit until you tell me why the fuck you're here in the middle of the night."

"I came to apologize for how I treated you. It was uncalled for and you didn't deserve it."

"I'm getting real tired of all your apologies, Law," she said, folding her arms.

I leaned against the back of the couch and looked her up and down. She looked gorgeous, even though she was mad at me. She tugged at her skirt after kicking off her heels at the doorway and walked past me into the kitchen. I stared at the way her body looked in that skirt and my dick started getting hard. Her titties sat up nice and perky and showed just the right amount of cleavage. It took everything in me not to bend her ass over the couch and fuck her right there. I stood and watched her grab a bottle of water out of the refrigerator and walk back into the bedroom, ignoring me.

"Raquel," I said, standing in the door of the bedroom.

"Why are you even still here, Law? We're done. You made that loud and clear when you tossed me out of your house on my ass!"

Raquel started to undress in front of me and change into her nightclothes. She put her hair into a bun and turned the sheets down.

"I'm not leaving until you accept my apology," I told her.

"Fine. I accept it. Whatever. Just get out," she said, pushing me out of the way.

I grabbed both of her arms and gently pushed her against the wall. I rested my forehead on hers and closed my eyes.

"Say it like you mean it."

"I forgive you, Law," she said with an attitude still in her voice.

I grabbed the sides of her face and kissed her. It didn't take long for her to kiss me back. I sucked on my middle finger and reached down inside her panties to rub her clit with it.

"Mmm, look at you. Already wet for me."

"Mmhm..." She moaned.

"Tell me you want this dick, Raquel."

"I want it..."

I picked her up and carried her to the bed. I hurriedly unbuckled my pants while she pulled off her panties and t-shirt. I put both of her legs above her head and slowly entered her. She screamed.

"Are you okay?"

"Just... just take it slow."

I leaned in to her and put her right leg over my left shoulder as I thrusted inside her. Then I kissed her.

"Oh my God. It's so fucking deep, Law." She moaned.

"Can you handle it, Raquel?"

"Mmhm... Fuck me, Law. Don't stop!"

She played with her nipples as I fucked her. I loved watching her titties jiggle as she stared deep into my eyes. I gave her a few more strokes and then pulled out of her and laid on my side. Raquel kept her right leg in the air as I entered her again. I let my hands massage her thighs as I dug into her and palmed her round ass.

"Goddamn, I love the way this pussy feels," I told her as I kissed her neck and shoulder.

I made sure my strokes were slow but deep. I wanted to make sure she felt every inch of me. I wrapped my arms around her as I gave her a good dick down. I missed the hell out of her, and I wanted to show her exactly how much.

"Turn over and let me hit it from the back," I instructed.

Raquel slowly turned over and got on all fours. I spread her ass cheeks apart and slid right inside her with ease. Her pussy had finally gotten used to my dick, but it still had a tight ass chokehold on it. I put my hand on her left shoulder and guided her back against my dick.

"That's it, Raquel. Fuck me back, baby."

"Mmmmmm... Shit! I'm about to cummmmm, baby!" she screamed as she pushed back against my dick.

"Shit, I'm about to nut, too," I told her.

It took everything inside me to pull out of her warm ass pussy, but I did, because I knew better. I headed to the bathroom, and then she went in after me.

"I really hate you, you know that?" she said from the bathroom.

"And why is that?" I asked.

"Because... you knew what you were doing when you came over here."

"I just wanted to show you how sorry I was." I smiled.

I glanced over at the edge of the bed and saw the iPhone I thought I'd smashed to pieces. I picked it up and wondered how she'd been using it. The screen looked like it would cut her fingers every time she touched it. I unlocked her phone while I heard water running in the bathroom and her camera roll was open. All the recent photos were taken months prior, which made me wonder how long she'd really had the phone and where she got it from in the first place. I clicked on her photos that were taken in Miami and immediately saw red. As soon as I saw her face, I went off.

"What the fuck are you still doing with this?" I yelled, holding up the phone.

"Law, what are you talking about? I already told you Shiya got me that phone!"

"I'm talking about this picture! How in the fuck do you still have it?"

"I... I don't know. I haven't looked at my photos or anything. I just logged into my iCloud account not too long ago!"

"Did you plan to take it to the police? Huh? Do you know what this shit could do to my family, Raquel, or me? Do you?"

"Law, listen. It must've been from my iCloud or something. I swear to God I would never do you like that! I didn't know it was even on there!" she said frantically.

"You know what? Shiya was right. I can't trust your ass. Fuck you, Raquel!"

I stormed out of the apartment and slammed the door behind me.

CHAPTER FIFTEEN
Blaze

I needed to get out of the house and get some new hos on my roster. The ones I'd been dealing with were getting stale and starting to nag, which told me I needed to recruit some new pussy. For a second, I thought I really might've been able to work things out between Raquel and I, but it didn't take a rocket scientist to see which Calloway brother she was really interested in. Law was just as interested in her too, although he never spoke on it.

"Where are you going all dressed up?" Nashiya asked me as I walked past her, heading toward the door.

"I'm headed out tonight. You know I can't deprive the ladies of all this Calloway goodness," I said, running my hand down my chest. "How are you feelin'?"

"You know you're a trip, right? But I'm doing better. I feel almost as good as new," she said, turning her wrist with the cast on it.

"Good enough to get you down the aisle though, right?" I asked.

"Nothing is going to stop me from getting down the aisle and marrying your brother," she assured me.

"That's what's up."

"Have fun tonight, and watch yourself messin' around with all those little nasty hos before you catch somethin' out there," she warned.

"Ah, don't worry about me, girl. I'm bulletproof," I assured her.

I headed back out to my favorite place, the strip club, with enough bands on me to feed a small village in a third-world country. As soon as I got to the club, I got a bottle of Hennessy and started pouring it out on bitches' asses and giving them a money shower at the same damn time. I was having the time of my life until I bumped into Darius.

"Yo, watch yourself, lil' nigga," he said as he bumped my shoulder.

"Watch who the fuck you talkin' to, nigga," I told him.

"Fuck you say to me?" he asked, stepping up to my face.

"I don't think I stuttered, mothafucka."

Darius reached out and pushed me, and I stumbled back. I tightened my grip around the bottle of liquor in my hand and smashed it over the back of his head. His boys and security rushed me at the same time, crashing into my body. I threw punches at anyone who came my way, just trying to get back to finish Darius's ass off. Out of nowhere, three gunshots rang out. All of the strippers screamed and ran as well as all the other people in the club, too. I continued to push forward until I felt a sharp pain jolt through my body. I looked over and realized I was bleeding from my shoulder. As soon as I saw the blood, the excruciating pain soon followed. I had been shot in the arm. I held my arm and ran out of the club. I didn't have my gun on me inside, so I made sure to keep it on my passenger seat as I drove just in case any of those niggas tried to get me in a drive-by situation. I was gonna shoot until the death of me.

I got home and made my way into the downstairs bathroom. I looked at my shirt, and it was soaked in the blood from the gunshot wound. I slowly peeled the shirt off my body and looked at my arm. I could see the bullet lodged in there. I ran some water on my hands and then tried to fish it out.

"Ahhhhhhhh, shit!" I groaned in pain.

I stood there with tears welling up in the corners of my eyes as I dug my finger inside my open wound. The pain was excruciating, but there was no way I was going to the hospital. I already knew the cops were all over the scene down at the strip club, and I didn't want to help their asses connect any dots.

"What the fuck happened to you?" Law said as he came in behind me.

"Goddamn, you scared me," I told him.

"Where have you been and what the fuck happened tonight, Blaze?" he said, closing the door behind him.

"I was out at the club doing my thing when I ran into Darius's bitch ass. He said some things. I said some things, and then he pushed me. I cracked a bottle over that nigga's skull, and then his boys and security rushed me at the same time. Before I could get to him, somebody shot me," I told him.

"Sit down," he instructed.

"Nah, I gotta get this fuckin' bullet out. I think I almost got it."

"No, you don't. You're only making it worse."

I sat down on the toilet and watched Law wash his hands. I turned so that my arm was facing him as he attempted to pull the bullet out of my arm.

"Ahhh fuck!" I yelled.

"Just sit still. I almost got it," he told me.

"Hurry up, nigga. This shit hurts!" I yelled.

Law maneuvered the bloody bullet out of my arm and tossed it in the sink. His hands were covered in my blood. He washed his hands again and then looked underneath the cabinet for something.

"I'll be right back."

Law returned with a bottle of vodka and poured some on my wound.

"Ahhhhhhhh shittttt! What the fuck, nigga!" I yelled as I smacked the bottle away from my arm.

"Do you wanna get an infection?" he asked, sternly.

I shook my head and tried to unscrew my face as the pain subsided.

"How'd you learn how to do this shit anyway?" I asked, clenching my jaw through the pain.

"Do what?"

"Get a bullet out."

"Dad taught me."

"Really? When?" I asked.

"It was years ago. I was probably in like middle school or something. He came home real late, and he was sitting in the living room. All I heard was moaning and groaning. At first, I thought somebody had broken into the house, so I got up, and peeked around the corner to check. That's when I saw him on the couch, digging in his arm. I never thought I'd actually be doin' the shit," he told me as he bandaged me up and looked at me.

"What?" I asked.

"Are you sure that's all that happened?" he asked.

"Yeah. That's all that happened."

"You gotta calm down, Blaze. You been acting real hot headed lately, and the shit might cost you your life if you're not careful."

"I'm not a baby no more, nigga. Don't worry about me. I'm a grown ass man. You ain't ever gotta question me, nigga. Especially not after all I've done for you."

"Everything I do is for you, nigga. Who the fuck are you tryna fool?" he asked.

I sighed.

"You're right. I ain't go out lookin' for trouble this time, but you know when it comes my way, I'ma handle it."

143

"Family takes care of one another. I already lost one brother. I can't lose you, too."

"Respect, man." I nodded.

"I love you, baby boy," he told me as he leaned down to kiss my forehead.

"Love you, too."

"Get some sleep. We gon' get at them niggas. Don't you worry," he assured me.

* * *

Ian

It seemed like the closer I got to my wedding, the more things started falling apart. My brother had just been shot, so that meant our little agreement with the Price family had went out the window. I was going to kill every last one of them, and that was on my father and my brother, Wolfe.

I walked back into my bedroom and took off my shirt that was stained with my brother's blood. I was thankful he was still alive. I couldn't handle losing another brother in the same year.

"What happened down there? I heard a lot of screaming."

"Everything is fine. Blaze... he got shot tonight.

"Oh my God. Is he okay?" Nashiya asked me.

"Yeah. He's going to be okay."

"Did he say who did it?"

"Nah," I lied.

"You already know who probably did it."

"Yeah, I do, but that don't got nothin' to do with you."

"Right. If it don't got nothin' to do with me, then who does it have to do with? Raquel?"

"What's that supposed to mean?" I asked. "You know what? Before you start, I don't even want to hear it," I snapped.

"Okay, damn. I'm sorry."

"Are you really, Shiya? Because it really don't seem that way to me."

"What do you mean by that, Law?"

"For one, why do you always bring Raquel up?"

"Excuse me?"

"Everything that happens you're quick to blame it on Raquel, or you're always dropping her name every chance you get."

"Because I told you I didn't trust her ass from the very beginning!"

"We are two fucking seconds away from this wedding, and all you can think about is her."

Nashiya sighed.

"I don't know what it's going to take for you to see that the bitch ain't good for us, baby."

"No good for us or no good for you?" I asked.

"You know what the fuck I mean! I told you she can't be trusted! If that's not enough for you, then I don't know what is. Shit, what else do you need? Her phone?"

"Wait. What? How'd you know she had a phone? I never told you I found that."

"Huh?"

"You heard me, Nashiya! How the fuck did you know about that shit?"

"It was just a guess, baby. I don't know for real."

"You don't fuckin' know or you do, Shiya? Which one is it?"

Nashiya sighed and looked at me. She couldn't even form her lips to make words come out. I shook my head as I looked at her with my nostrils flaring. Her slip up was all I needed to hear. I turned my back and headed straight for the door.

"Law, baby, wait!" she yelled.

I let the door slam behind me and kept walking. I never thought that Nashiya would be the one to try and sabotage me, and there I was taking the shit out on Raquel again. All that shit had my mind so fucked up. I didn't know what or who to believe.

CHAPTER SIXTEEN
Nashiya

Not only had I put my foot in my mouth, but I had shoved it all the way down my fuckin' throat. When Law stormed out of the room, all I saw was my future going right down the drain quicker than I could spell marriage. I quickly grabbed my phone off the nightstand and called Dallas.

"Hello?" he answered.

"What the fuck did you do?" I growled.

"What are you talking about?"

"I told you to keep that bitch occupied, didn't I?"

"And I am. I just saw her. What the fuck do you want me to do? Move in? What's the urgency anyway?" he asked.

"Don't worry about it. Just do what the fuck you told me you were going to do, Dallas!"

"Don't you worry your pretty little head about it. I got you. You just sit back and let daddy work his magic," he said and hung up.

* * *

Raquel

What Law and I shared between us was the sweetest kind of murder. One look from him, and it felt like my entire world came crashing down. But that didn't give him the right to treat me the way he did and flip on me at the drop of a dime. I was laying down when my phone rang. I looked at the cracked screen and realized it was Dallas calling me. I almost didn't answer it, but decided I didn't have anything to lose.

"Hello?"

"What's going on, miss?"

"Just laying here. What about you?"

"Would you like some company?"

I took the phone away from my ear and looked at the time. It was almost 11:00 p.m.

"Um, it's kind of late."

"C'mon, miss. You've been avoiding me for a couple days. I tried to play it off at first, but now I'm really starting to take offense." He chuckled.

I laughed along with him.

"Okay. Fine."

I jumped up, got in the shower, and put my hair in a slick, high ponytail. I threw on a pair of black joggers, a white tank top, and a pair of fuzzy socks. Dallas shot me a text and told me he was downstairs. I went downstairs to get him and brought him back up.

"Wow. So, this is how you livin', huh?"

"More like housesitting."

"Damn, I need me a nice little set up like this," he said as he walked into the living room and sat down.

"So you're here," I said as I smiled at him.

"In the flesh, baby. Did you miss me?"

"Um..."

"You don't have to answer that. I already know." He laughed.

"Whatever, boy."

"Can I at least get a hug and a kiss?"

"A hug and a kiss? Boy, who do you think you are? My man or somethin'?" I asked.

"Hey, I'm always gonna shoot my shot." He laughed again.

"You can get a hug and maybe a peck if you act right."

"A peck, huh?"

"Yeah, nigga. A peck."

"I'll take that."

The two of us stood up, and I wrapped my arms around his neck as he bent down to hug me. As soon as I tried to pull away, he leaned down and kissed me deeply as his hands moved down from my face to the sides of my neck and over my shoulders. Dallas's hand made it all the way down my body, stopping at my pussy, and he rubbed it.

"Hey, wait..." I said, moving back from him.

Dallas smiled.

"I'm sorry... I just can't get enough of you, beautiful."

I looked in his eyes and smiled at him. He kissed my neck as he rubbed my pussy through my pants again. I could feel myself getting wetter and wetter. I started panting like a dog in the summer time. He put his hand down my panties and rubbed my clit, then licked his finger.

"I just want to taste you, Raquel," he whispered in my ear.

"Dallas, I..."

"Shh," he said, placing his finger over my lips. "We don't have to do anything you're uncomfortable with, but I promise you'll like it. Just relax."

We sat down, and I let Dallas kiss me again and lay my back against the couch. He moved from my lips, to my neck and down to kiss my breasts through my tank top. He slowly lifted my shirt so that he could kiss my belly button, and then slowly started to spread my legs. His hands glided up my thighs and stopped when he came to my clit. I felt him apply pressure with his right thumb and then move it around in small circles.

"Mmm..." I moaned.

"Feels good, doesn't it?" he asked.

I nodded.

"Real good."

Dallas lifted the lower half of my body and pulled my pants and panties down at the same time.

"Are you going to let me taste you tonight, Raquel?"

"Mmhm." I nodded, while biting my bottom lip.

Dallas flashed me a devious smile before lifting my legs up in the air and placing himself right in between.

"Damn your pussy is beautiful," he told me.

He buried his face in between my legs and kissed my pussy lips and my clit gently. I squirmed like a fish out of water. His soft lips felt so good. I threw my head back in ecstasy.

"Mmm... I knew you'd taste as good as you looked," he said, flicking my clit with his long tongue.

I sat up on my elbows and watched him dine. He moved his head from left to right in a mix of slow and fast motion. He spread my pussy lips and licked my clit. With every lick, my breaths got shorter and choppier.

"Oooh shit!" I squealed.

I could feel my stomach tense up as I tried to remember to breathe. I felt like bullet holes were in my lungs. It was so hard to breathe. The closer I got to my climax, my body instinctively started moving in slow circles against his face.

"Mmm, fuck!" I said as I gripped the back of his head, taking hold of a handful of his crinkly dreads.

I held both sides of his head in my hands as I watched him feast on me as if I was the last meal he'd ever have. I could feel myself started to explode, so I pulled his head back up and kissed him. Dallas swirled his tongue around in my mouth and smiled.

"You liked it?" he asked.

"Very much." I nodded, still trying to catch my breath.

"Mmm... Then let me finish, beautiful."

"No. I don't think I can handle it."

"Let me finish eatin' your sweet ass pussy, Raquel."

Dallas lowered himself back in between my legs, kissed my inner thighs, and then each pussy lip gently. He ran this tongue up and down the side and then sucked on my clit. All my muscles seemed to tighten up at once and then released as I came.

"Mmm... That's right. Cum all on my tongue, Raquel."

"Mmmmmm shiiiiiitttttt!" I screamed in pure pleasure as I came.

"Goddamn, you taste good as hell," he said as he wiped his mouth.

My legs were shaking uncontrollably as I rode the wave of my orgasm. It was my first time having an orgasm from having my pussy licked. Derrick used to do it when we were together, but he could never make me cum. Dallas had the tongue of a god. All I could do was lay there and listen to my erratic breathing.

"Damn, daddy tongue game got you stuck, huh?" He smirked.

"Shut up." I laughed.

"You know you just fell in love, girl, don't front," he laughed.

"Whatever!"

As soon as I said that, Dallas's phone rang. He pulled it out of his pocket and looked at the caller ID and then pressed ignore.

"Important?" I asked.

"Nah. It's not. You're more important than any phone call right now."

I smiled and stood up to put my panties and pants back on and heard a knock at my door.

"You expecting someone?" he asked.

"No. Actually, I'm not," I said as I walked over to look through the peephole.

Dallas followed behind me and stood there.

"Shit," I mumbled.

"What's wrong? Who is it? You need me to get them to go away?"

"No. I got it. Just go back in the living room. I'll only be a second."

"Are you sure?"

"Yeah. I'm positive. I got this."

Dallas walked back into the living room, and I unlocked the door, cracking it open.

"What do you want?" I asked as I stood face to face with Law.

"Can you let me in first?"

"No."

"I need to talk to you."

"Whatever you have to say, you can say it right here."

"Raquel..."

"I'm serious. I'm done with your shit."

"Can you at least open the door and let me in?"

"Now's not a good time. I—I have company."

"Excuse me?"

"You heard me. I've got company."

Law pushed open the door, knocking me out of the way. He scanned the apartment until his eyes landed on Dallas. He walked over to him, pulled him up by his shirt, and slammed his body into the hard ground. He landed two punches to his face. Dallas rolled over on top of him and punched him back. I stood over them, screaming for the both of them to stop.

"I better not ever see you around her again, or I'll kill you, nigga. I swear to fucking God!" Law yelled as he dragged Dallas by his hair towards the front door. Dallas stood to his feet and shoved Law backwards. Law tackled him, and they both hit the ground again and started tussling.

"Stop! Fucking stop right now!" I yelled.

Law and Dallas both stood up, and Law pushed him out of the front door and slammed it behind him.

"Oh my God, Law. What the fuck is wrong with you!" I said, slapping him repeatedly in the back with all the strength I had in me.

Law held the sides of his head like he was going crazy. His eyes were bloodshot red.

"Not you too, Raquel."

"What are you talking about? You're not making any sense."

"Do you know who that was?"

"Yeah, his name is Dallas. We've been seeing each other for a couple weeks now."

"Dallas fucking Price, Raquel? I swear to God I don't know who to trust!"

"What are you talking about? What's wrong with him?" I asked, reaching out for his arm.

Law quickly snatched it away.

"Don't you fucking touch me!"

"Law, I just need you to calm down and tell me what the fuck is going on, okay? I can't help you unless you tell me."

"Help me? You and that bitch Shiya are setting me up!"

"Hold up. What? Me and Shiya? Now I know you're crazy. First, she thinks I'm trying to kill her, and now, you think that I'm working with her to set you up? What the fuck is really going on?"

"His brother shot Blaze in the arm, Raquel! His family killed Wolfe! And you're just over here sleeping with my fucking enemy! He's using you as a pawn to get back at me! He doesn't want you!"

I put my hand over my mouth and immediately felt sick to my stomach. I closed my eyes and had flashback after flashback. The first was meeting Dallas in the first place the night I was

153

kidnapped, the second was randomly seeing him again the day I was out with Nashiya and how she seemed to be pushing me straight into his arms. The third was a few minutes before Law arrived at my house. Dallas's phone started blowing up. Whoever it was wanted to talk to him really bad, but he wouldn't answer around me.

"Oh my God! Law, I—I don't know what to say. I didn't know. I swear!"

"I swear to God I want to kill everybody!" he yelled as he smacked a glass onto the kitchen floor.

"What does Shiya have to do with any of this?"

"I don't know who to trust anymore."

"You can trust me, Law."

Law glanced up at me and shook his head.

"Tell you the truth, I haven't felt like myself in months," he said.

"And why is that?"

"I don't know."

"Well what do you know?" I asked.

Law sighed and shook his head again.

"Nothing apparently... I can't even trip. A part of me knew what I was getting myself into when I proposed to that bitch. She slipped up tonight and told me about your phone."

"So now you believe me?"

"I came here to apologize, but when I saw Dallas here, I didn't know what to think."

"I would've never had him over here or anywhere near me had I known that his family was the one that you were having problems with. I'm not that type of person."

"I think I know that now." He nodded.

"So, what are you going to do? You know... about your wedding and everything?"

"I don't know."

"Are you still going to go through with it? You can't seriously still be considering that."

"I said I don't know what I'm going to do. All I know is I'm not going to let these niggas keep fuckin' with my family."

"Aren't you afraid they're going to retaliate? First, Blaze and his brother, and now, this situation that just happened here tonight?"

"I don't give a fuck about none of that, Raquel. If they do, I'll be ready to go to war. Our families have been fighting for years. Ain't nothing changed. I'll still die for mine whenever that time comes."

"Okay." I nodded. "You can stay here tonight if you want."

"I'm not laying my head nowhere that nigga has been. I'm going home," he said and left.

CHAPTER SEVENTEEN

Nashiya

I sat up and waited all night for Law to come home. My heart skipped a beat when he came through the bedroom door at 8:00 a.m.

"Law... baby."

He threw his hand up to silence me, walked straight into the bathroom, and closed the door behind him. I needed him to forgive me and give me a chance to explain myself. I crawled out of bed, undressed, and walked into the bathroom. Law had already stepped inside the shower, and I slid open the door to step in behind him. Without saying a word, I wrapped my arms around his waist and laid my ear against his back.

"C'mon, Shiya. Get off me."

"Law, baby, I'm sorry..."

"I don't want to talk about shit. I just want to shower alone, aight?"

"Okay." I nodded. "We don't have to talk."

I reached around, ran my good hand down his hard, wet chest, and then made my way down to his dick. I wrapped my hand around it and slowly started jacking him off to get him hard.

"Shiya, stop," he said, moving my hand.

"I just want to make you feel good, baby."

"I'm good. I told you what I wanted to do, and this ain't part of that. Now, move."

Law had never rejected me like that before. I didn't know what to do. The only thing I could think of was to try again until he gave in. I knew he was mad at me, but damn. I exhaled deeply, cracked my neck, and then dropped down to my knees. I turned him around and took his semi-hard dick in my hand, licked around the tip, and then put it in my warm mouth. I could feel it getting harder with every lick.

"Shiya..."

I could hear it in his voice that he was enjoying my head, so I kept going. I didn't care that my weave or my cast were getting wet. All I wanted to do was please my man. Law gripped the back of my head and slowly started moving his dick in and out of my mouth. If I could've smiled then, I would've. *Got 'em*, I thought. I made sure to keep my mouth as wet and warm as the water coming out of the showerhead. Law pushed my head deeper onto his dick, and I relaxed my throat to let his dick slide all the way in my mouth then came up for air before he did it again.

"Oooh shit." He groaned, pulling my hair.

"Mmm... You like that, baby?"

"Mmhm."

The soap from his body dripped down onto mine, making my breasts soapy. I smacked his dick against my hard, wet nipples, and put his dick in between my large breasts and let him titty fuck me for a second. Then I kissed up the side of it and sucked on the tip like a lollipop. I licked up and down the shaft as I sucked the sides. I lifted his dick up and sucked on his balls as I twisted my good wrist around his shaft.

"Mmm... shit... just like that!"

"Mmm... I love your dick, baby," I said as I smeared his dick across my lips.

"You love this dick, Shiya?"

157

"Yes, baby. I do."

I smacked his dick against my tongue and continued to deep throat him while making sure to make the head as sloppy as possible.

"Ahhh shit!" He groaned.

I licked up the side of his dick as cum squirted out the tip like a water fountain. I sucked the rest of the cum off his dick and kissed the tip. I stood back up and reached up to kiss him, but he turned his head. Without saying a word, he turned back around and continued washing his body.

* * *

I was still mad as hell at Nashiya, but I needed the release. I had spent the rest of the night driving, smoking, and thinking when I left from seeing Raquel. I figured out whose side Nashiya was really on, and she was going to have to be dealt with. I knew exactly what I was going to do moving forward, and I didn't plan to tell anyone about it. The only person I knew I could fully trust was myself.

"Are you ready for tomorrow, bruh?" Blaze asked me.

"Yeah." I shrugged. "I guess so."

"Just say the word, man, and I can shut it down."

"Nah, I got it. Trust me," I assured him.

I still hadn't talked to Raquel, but I knew that I wanted her present for my big day, so I decided to put the bug in Blaze's ear.

"Yo, you talked to Raquel lately?"

"Nah. I swung by there to throw some groceries in the crib for her, but that's about it. Why? What's up?"

"I want her to come tomorrow."

"Hold up. You want her to come tomorrow... to your wedding... and watch you marry the woman who hates her?"

"I know it sounds fucked up, but it's what I want. Can you just make sure she's there?"

"Yeah, bruh, I got you." He nodded.

When I woke up on my wedding day, I expected to feel happy and secure to know that I was marrying a loyal woman who would never lie to me, but that wasn't the case. I hadn't seen Shiya since she topped me off in the shower the day before. The next time I'd be seeing her was when she was walking down the aisle to become Mrs. Andreas Calloway.

I got up and got dressed, making sure I was looking my Sunday best, and headed to the church. I was sitting in the back, tucking my gun in the back of my pants, when Blaze came in with his bowtie undone around his neck.

"What's up? You good?" he asked.

"Yeah, I'm good."

"Nigga, what was you doin' back here? Prayin'?" he joked.

I chuckled.

"Nah, just thinking."

"Thinkin' about what?" he asked as he stood in the mirror and adjusted and fastened his bowtie.

"Nothin'. It's nothin'," I said, shaking my head.

"I know you lyin', so I'm just going to leave you to it. You know where to find me if you need me."

"Is Raquel out there?"

"Yeah. I got her here kicking and screaming, but she's here."

"Thanks." I nodded.

Blaze stepped back and looked at me.

"What's really going on in that head of yours, Law?"

"I told you it's nothin'."

"Aight. Well, the wedding is about to start in a few minutes, so we best get out there."

"Okay, I'll be out in a second."

"Love you, bruh."

"Love you, too, youngin'."

Blaze stood alongside me when the ceremony started. I watched Nashiya's bridesmaids walk down the aisle, followed by the flower girls, and then her. She looked beautiful. There was no denying that. I quickly scanned the church for Raquel and found her in the back corner. We locked eyes for a second, and she quickly diverted her eyes away from me. I focused my attention back on Nashiya, who had stopped smiling at me.

"Dearly beloved, we are gathered here today to join Andreas and Nashiya together as one in holy matrimony. If there is anyone here who has just cause as to why these two should not be joined in holy matrimony, speak now or forever hold your peace."

The church fell silent as the two of us looked at each other. She smiled at me and then looked back at the reverend.

"We will proceed with the vows. Nashiya, we will start with you."

Nashiya cleared her throat, handed her flowers to one of her girls standing behind her, and grabbed both of my hands.

"Law, I've waited for this day since the first moment I met you. I always knew that you would be my husband. I wanna thank you, baby, for... for... just being loyal to me and choosing to love me and picking me to be your wife and bear your children so that the Calloway name can live on. I know that I'm not perfect, but you love me anyway. I love you," she said, wiping her eyes.

I reached out and wiped her tears. She kissed the palm of my hand. The preacher then gave me a head nod, which let me know it was my turn.

"Shiya, it's been five years, and from the moment I met you, I knew you were different. I wanted nothing more than to give you the world in exchange for your loyalty, but now I know that you're not the woman I thought you were. You could've cost me everything, and now your actions have cost you everything," I said as I put my hand behind my back.

Nashiya snatched her hand away from mine and looked at me.

"Law, what are you saying?"

"I'm saying, I'm not marrying you today, Shiya. I'm not marrying you ever. The wedding is off," I said as I took my hand off the gun in my pants and loosened my tie.

The entire crowd gasped as Shiya stood frozen in front of me. Her lips trembled as her face broke up into a million pieces and tears started flowing down her face.

"H—how could you do this to me?"

"You did this to yourself, now you gotta live with the consequences."

"I hate you!" she screamed and then slapped me hard across the face.

She turned her back to me and ran out of the church crying with her girls all following closely behind her.

CHAPTER EIGHTEEN

Raquel

I couldn't believe my eyes or my ears. Law had really called off his marriage to Nashiya at the damn wedding. I wanted to jump for joy and shout to the heavens, but I remained seated. When the majority of the guests started shuffling out of the church, I walked over to Law who was sitting in the front pew.

"So that was your big, bright idea?"

"Yeah." He nodded slowly.

"You sure know how to bring the dramatics."

"I know, right?" He shrugged.

"How do you feel?"

"Like I finally made the right decision."

"That's a good feeling..."

"Look, Raquel, I'm sorry about everything, okay? I really am."

"I'm sorry, too."

"And if you still want to leave and go back to your old life... I won't stop you."

"Wow," I said.

I had been yearning to hear those words for months, and when I finally did, they didn't sound as sweet.

"What?"

"I never thought I'd actually hear you say it..."

"Well, I just did. I'll take you to the airport right now and buy you a ticket for wherever it is you want to go. You deserve to get the fuck out of Miami. Shit, if it wasn't for all the shit I had going on, I'd probably leave this mothafuckin' city, too."

I watched as Law leaned over, rested his elbows on his knees, and clasped his hands together. Although we both knew he'd made the right decision, I could tell he had mixed feelings about it. He really did care for Nashiya, and for her to set him up like that really cut him deeper than any of us thought it had.

"I would take you up on your offer. It's just if I left, I'd be leaving my heart here in Miami... with you."

Law looked up at me with a blank look on his face.

"What are you saying?"

"I'm saying... although I didn't plan on it, I fell in love with you, Law."

* * *

Hearing Raquel tell me she loved me sounded so genuine and beautiful coming out of her mouth, but I just couldn't bring myself to say it back. Even though I knew I felt it, the last bitch I'd said it to had burned me in the worst way possible. I couldn't handle another upset like that right away. I knew in my heart that a thousand armies couldn't keep me away from Raquel, but I was smarter than that. There was going to be a war soon. I could feel it. I had to hide my feelings for her safety, no matter how much it was killing me inside.

"C'mon. Let's get out of here."

"Wait. Did you hear me?" she asked.

"I did." I nodded.

"And you're not going to say it back?"

"I just... I just went through a lot of stuff, and I'm just not trying to jump out of one situation into another one."

"Wow..."

I could tell she was hurt, and that's the last thing I wanted to do, but I knew it would hurt more if I lied to her.

"I'm sorry, Raquel."

"Nah, it's fine. This whole thing was stupid of me anyway. I never should've fucking said anything." She huffed.

Raquel started speed walking down the aisle to the entrance of the church, and I was right on her heels.

"Raquel, wait up!"

Right when we walked out of the church, four cop cars surrounded us with at least eight cops pointing guns at us. We both stopped dead in our tracks.

"Freeze! Put your hands up!"

I looked over at Raquel, and we both slowly put our hands up. It was no secret that cops didn't have to have a reason to shoot someone, especially when they were black. Two cops walked over to us.

"Andreas Calloway, you are under arrest for the murder of Damien Price."

"Hold up. What?"

One cop pulled Raquel to the side, while the other placed cuffs around my wrists and escorted me to the back of a cop car. I could hear Raquel screaming for them to let me go in the background, but the officer reading me my Miranda Rights took precedence in my ear.

"You have the right to remain silent. Anything you say can and will be used against you in a court of law..."

To Be Continued...

Afterword

Readers,

Thanks for following along with me on my literary journey so far. Also, thank you for reading *In the Arms of a Savage*. Got a second to leave a review? If you've made it this far, I hope you'll consider taking a minute to tell me what you thought about the book. I thoroughly enjoy reading them! Why does this matter? I'm always striving to attract new readers and retain current ones, and reviews are one of the easiest ways to attract readers. If you loved the book, tell a friend, and most importantly, let me know!

Thanks so much,

K.L. Hall

Other books by K.L. Hall:

About the author.

K.L. Hall is a national bestselling and award-winning author. As a serial storyteller, Hall has penned over three dozen titles in various genres—including African American urban fiction and romance, paranormal, children's books (as Kimberley M.), and non-fiction. Her fictional stories straddle the intersection of classic Urban and spell-binding Romance.

Highly Acclaimed Titles:

In the Arms of a Savage: (Peaked at #1 in Women's Fiction)

The Potomac Falls Series (Peaked at #1 and #2 in African American Erotica)

Sign up for my mailing list to stay updated with new releases, giveaways, sneak peeks, and more! Click this link: https://bit.ly/38RMpV5

Connect with me on social media:

Facebook: https://www.facebook.com/authorklhall

Twitter: https://twitter.com/authorklhall

Instagram: https://www.instagram.com/officialklhall/

Website: https://www.authorklhall.com .

Other novels by K.L. Hall:

Diary of a Hood Princess 1-3

Rise of a Street King: The Justice Silva Story *(Spin-Off to the Diary of a Hood Princess series)*

Broken Condoms and Promises 1-3

In the Arms of a Savage 1-3

Built for a Savage: Blaze and Camille's Love Story *(Spin-Off to the In the Arms of a Savage Series)*

A Ruthle$$ Love Story 1-3

Fallin' for the Alpha of the Streets 1-2

The Most Savage of Them All: The Wolfe Calloway Story *(Prequel to the In the Arms of a Savage Series)*

When a Gangsta Loves a Good Girl

Caught Between My Husband and a Hustler

The Illest Taboo 1-2

To the Only Thug I'll Ever Love

A Lover's Heist: Chief and Gianna's Love Story

A Lover's Heist II: Rome and Lira's Love Story

A Lover's Heist III: Baby and Skai's Love Story

Crushed Velvet & Cashmere

Crushed Velvet & Cashmere 2

Entanglements

Never Had a Bad Boy Love Me So Good

Good Girls Always Got a Thing for the Thugs

Professor Zaddy: A Potomac Falls Novel

Bound in the Arms of a Thug: Chop & Kendyl's Love Story

Make Mine a Gangsta: The Patton Brothers Book One

Gimme a Gangsta: The Patton Brothers Book Two

In The Arms of a Savage 1-3

Short Reads + Novellas:

Bi-Curious: An Erotic Tale

Bi-Curious 2: Tastes Like Candy

A Savage Calloway Christmas *(Christmas novella to the In the Arms of a Savage Series)*

Lovin' the Alpha of the Streets: A Valentine's Day Novella *(Valentine's Day novella to the Fallin' for the Alpha of the Streets Series)*

Awakened: A Paranormal Romance

As Long as You Stay Down

Solace in Seven

Solace II: The Final Cut

Something Bleu

Something Borrowed

Something New

The Knight Before Christmas: A Potomac Falls Short

I'll Be Home for Christmas: A Potomac Falls Short Book II

Triggered: A Potomac Falls Novella

Wasted Off You: A Friends to Lovers Novella

Because You Don't Know My Name: A Potomac Falls Novella

Will You Say My Name: A Potomac Falls Novella Book Two

Remember My Name: A Potomac Falls Novella Book Three

Every Thug Needs a Lady: A Lady and the Tramp Retelling

Ten Things I Hate About Lovin' You: An Enemies to Lovers Novella

In Exchange: An Urban Thriller

T.A.N.: An Erotic Novella

A Gangsta's Love Language: A Patton Brothers Spin-Off

Children's Books:

Princess for Hire

Princess Twinkle Toes & the Missing Magic Sneakers

Little One, Change the World

Adjust Your Crown: A Self-Love Coloring Book for Children of Color

Non-Fiction:

Authors are a Business: The Booked & Busy Course Mini Book

Connect with me on Social Media:

Facebook: K.L. Hall https://goo.gl/yGP59B

Twitter: @authorklhall

Instagram: @authorklhall

Website: www.authorklhall.com

Sign up for my mailing list to stay up to date with new releases, giveaways, and more here: goo.gl/l6IMUp